PENGU

FORGET ME NOT, STRANGER

Novoneel Chakraborty is the author of fifteen bestsellers, two novellas and one short-story collection. His works have been translated into multiple Indian languages. His Forever series made it to the *Times of India*'s Most Stunning Books of 2017. His latest, *Roses Are Blood Red*, is still on the list of top ten books across India even nine months after its release. His twists, dark plots and strong female protagonists have earned him the moniker 'Sidney Sheldon of India'.

The first book in the Stranger trilogy, which became a phenomenal hit among young adults, has been adapted into a web series, *Hello Mini*, on MX Player, produced by Applause Entertainment and Rose Movies. The show already has more than 100 million views. His erotic thriller novel *Black Suits You* has been adapted into a hit web series, titled *Bekaaboo*, by Alt Balaji. His novella *Red Suits You* is all set to be adapted as well.

Apart from novels, Novoneel has written and developed several hit TV and web shows for premier channels like Sony, Star Plus and Zee. He lives and works in Mumbai.

NOVONEEL CHAKRABORTY

FORGET ME NOT, STRANGER

Penguin
metro reads

An imprint of Penguin Random House

PENGUIN METRO READS

USA | Canada | UK | Ireland | Australia
New Zealand | India | South Africa | China

Penguin Metro Reads is part of the Penguin Random House group of companies
whose addresses can be found at global.penguinrandomhouse.com

Published by Penguin Random House India Pvt. Ltd
7th Floor, Infinity Tower C, DLF Cyber City,
Gurgaon 122 002, Haryana, India

First published by Random House India in 2016
Published in Penguin Metro Reads by Penguin Random House India 2020

Copyright © Novoneel Chakraborty 2016

16 15 14 13 12

ISBN 9788184007305

This is a work of fiction. Names, characters, places and incidents are either the
product of the author's imagination or are used fictitiously and any resemblance
to any actual person, living or dead, events or locales is entirely coincidental.

Typeset in Requiem Text by Manipal Digital Systems, Manipal
Printed at Thomson Press India Ltd, New Delhi

www.penguin.co.in

For . . .

The two souls I can't name.
One happens to be the most prized experience of my life.
The other, the most significant event.

Three things can't be long hidden:
the sun, the moon and the truth

The Buddha

Prologue

She was lost in the dark, dense forest. It was worse since she wasn't alone. Someone was following her, and had been for quite some time.

Her eyes were used to the darkness by now. She kept running, unsure of the direction. She had not seen the face of the person she was running from but she had an eerie feeling she would be cornered the moment she stopped. And so she ran, even though her legs were about to give way. She paused for a moment to catch her breath, and turned to look. Some dead leaves crackled in the distance and fear woke up in her guts once again.

Rivanah Bannerjee started running again. She checked her phone for the umpteenth time but there was still no network. She quickly checked the messages she had sent Danny. None of them had been delivered yet. She couldn't even shout for help because, for one, there was nobody in the forest and, two, it would only alert her follower and help track her down all the more easily. Just as she was about to collapse from exhaustion, Rivanah noticed a light in the distance. From where she was standing, Rivanah couldn't say what the source of the light was. But a light in the middle of the forest gave her hope. She took a deep breath and ran towards it with gusto. As she approached the light, she saw that it was inside what looked like an abandoned house. A huge banyan tree had spread its branches all over the wooden house—like a curse hanging above it.

When she reached the house, she peeped in through the window. Her breathing slowly regained a normal pace. There were four lanterns, one at each corner of the room, giving it a hauntingly erotic ambience. The room was barely furnished otherwise.

Right in the middle of the room was a naked man on his knees with his back to her. Around the man's neck were wrapped two shapely female legs. The man's mouth was right between the girl's legs. The girl suddenly popped her head up—her eyes were rolled back in ecstasy. As Rivanah got a good look of the girl's face, her heart stopped. She was staring at her own image! The Rivanah who was clutching the man's hair with both hands suddenly looked directly at the Rivanah peeping in through the window.

'Hello, Hiya!' the Rivanah inside the house said to the one outside. The man paused for a moment but didn't turn. He slowly held her throat with both hands and said aloud, 'Death is the ultimate orgasm, Mini.' He tightened his grip on her throat. Rivanah started to lose her senses. She could feel the pressure of the man's hands choking her windpipe. She tried to break free but couldn't. There was nobody who could help her except for her own 'image' standing by the window, helpless. The Rivanah at the window felt her feet turn to ice. She desperately wanted to escape. She felt her breath becoming shorter as if the man was pressing her throat instead of the girl's inside. An acute survival instinct finally gave her the energy to move. Rivanah went around the house looking for the main door. When she found it, she couldn't push it open. She banged hard, kicked it a few times but it wouldn't budge. The Rivanah inside the house was choking. The kicks on the door were relentless now and grew more intense. Finally the door crashed open and Rivanah ran towards the man who was holding the naked Rivanah by her throat. Before she could reach him, the man turned around to face her.

She opened her eyes wide. All she could see was a whitewashed ceiling with a static white fan. She saw Danny lying by her side, his face turned away from her. For a moment Rivanah thought she was still in her nightmare. She forcibly turned Danny's face towards her. She relaxed.

'What happened?' Danny asked in a sleepy voice.

'Nothing,' Rivanah said, feeling guilty for having disturbed his sleep. It was a nightmare, after all—a super-weird one all right, but a nightmare nevertheless.

'Go back to sleep,' she said. Danny obediently closed his eyes.

A quick look at her phone told her it was 10.45 in the night. Rivanah was about to get up to fetch some water when she heard a bell ring a couple of times. She ambled to the window and noticed an ice-cream wallah within the building premises. A family of four was buying ice creams from him. The sight made her miss her college days when Ekansh, her ex-boyfriend, would come over to her place at midnight and together they would have ice creams from a particular joint run by Ekansh's friend. Though the thought of Ekansh made her feel sour, a sudden urge to have ice cream possessed her. One look at Danny and his open mouth and soft snores told her he wouldn't come along. She picked up her wallet and quietly slipped out of the flat.

She bought herself a bar of khatta-meetha-aam-flavoured ice cream. After finishing one, she bought another to take back to her flat. By then the family of four had gone. Taking the money from Rivanah, the ice-cream wallah too turned to make an exit from the building premises.

As Rivanah walked towards her building entrance, there was a loud splash. Somebody had thrown a bucketful of water on her from above. Drenched from head to toe, she angrily looked up to reprimand the culprit but saw no one.

'Asshole!' she screamed out. There was a strange smell emanating from her clothes. She sniffed—and stopped dead in her tracks. What she had mistaken for water was, in fact, kerosene! Rivanah looked up again. Something like an arrow was travelling fast towards her. A flaming arrow.

'Oh my God!' she gasped, knowing well it wasn't a dream any more. The smell of the kerosene was real. The fire was real. She was real. Her fear was real. Rivanah had only a few seconds to move before the fiery missile touched her and burnt her to the ground. But her feet seemed to have frozen with fear. Just like in the nightmare. As the fireball neared her, her mind had already started a countdown—5—4—3—2 . . .

1

'Hey, you should call Aunty back. She has already called thrice,' Ishita said once Rivanah came out of the shower.

'I don't know why Mumma keeps worrying even though I'm in Kolkata, my hometown,' Rivanah said, picking up her phone. Rivanah was feeling sick ever since she had come back to Ishita's PG from Hiya's house in Agarpara. She could feel fear flutter in her guts. *Will the stranger really kill her? Was he a stalker cum serial killer?*

Ishita had been coaxing Rivanah to eat something but she didn't feel like it. Rivanah tried to sleep but feared that when she opened her eyes, she would see the stranger standing right in front of her, waiting to kill her. *Just like he must have compelled Hiya Chowdhury to kill herself,* she thought. Ishita had asked her to take a long, warm shower in order to relax. It sounded like a good idea. And now that she was done with the shower, Rivanah was indeed better.

'Hello, Mumma, what happened?' She finally called her mother back.

'Mini, come home. Now!' Her mother sounded petrified.

Rivanah's heart skipped a beat. Something terrible must have happened.

'What's wrong, Mumma?' Rivanah sounded equally terrified.

There was no response for a moment and then her mother said calmly, 'Nothing. I'm just feeling lonely. Come home now, Mini!'

This was strange. Suddenly her mother sounded as if everything was all right. 'You scared me, Mumma. Anyway, I'm coming home. And I'm bringing Ishita along.'

'No, not now,' Mrs Bannerjee shot back instantly.

'Why?'

'We have to go out for lunch to your baba's colleague's place.'

'Today?'

'Yes, today. In fact, in a few hours. So come home immediately.'

'Okay, Mumma. I'm coming.' *Why did her mother sound so . . . unlike herself?*

'What happened?' Ishita asked, entering the room with two cups of green tea. She gave one to Rivanah.

'No, thanks. I need to go now. Have a luncheon to attend,' Rivanah said, combing her hair in front of a full-length mirror in the room.

'With Ekansh?'

Rivanah shot her a glance and sighed, 'Baba's colleague.'

'Okay, I get it,' Ishita said, sipping her green tea. Rivanah shrugged.

'Your mother wants to introduce you to another of your arranged-marriage guys.'

Rivanah rolled her eyes realizing Ishita was right. How could she have missed that?

'Wish me luck,' Rivanah said, and left.

A few hours later, Rivanah's father met her and her mother outside the Esplanade metro station, and they drove in his Alto to Kalikapur. Rivanah didn't say much during the journey. It was obvious in the way her mother had asked her to 'dress properly' while she herself wore her latest buy—a Baluchari sari. They could try but Rivanah had no intention of getting married just yet. She was sure her parents hadn't told her the real reason for the luncheon fearing she wouldn't go with them.

The Bannerjee family were received warmly by Manick Dutta on their arrival.

'So nice to see you, Mr Bannerjee,' he said, hugging Rivanah's father. Rivanah thought it was odd that he referred to her father by his surname. Generally all his colleagues addressed him by his first name.

'It's been a while since I met your family,' Mr Dutta added.

Been a while? When did he meet Mumma and me? Rivanah wondered. *He must be confusing us with someone else,* she thought. Soon all of them settled on a spacious L-shaped couch. It was a posh and neatly kept flat.

'My wife and son will be here soon. They have gone to the AC market. As you already know, Rishabh is here only for a week, and his mother prefers shopping with him.'

So his name is Rishabh—the man my parents want me to spend the rest of my life with. She noticed a couple of family photos in frames on either side of the huge LED television. Mr Dutta's son looked much older than she was. *If that is really his son in the photograph*, she thought and casually glanced at Mr Dutta. He was smiling at her.

'How are you doing, Mini?'

Calling me by my nickname when we are meeting for the first time? This is a first, thought Rivanah.

'I'm good, uncle. How are you?' Rivanah said, maintaining a warm smile.

'I'm good too. How long will you be in Kolkata?'

'A few more days.'

'That's nice.'

A servant came in with a tray carrying three glasses of water. The Bannerjees took a glass each and sipped on the water idly, waiting for Mr Dutta's wife and son to return. In the meantime, Mr Dutta shot a volley of questions at Rivanah. It was evident from the nature of the questions that he wanted to judge her as a person.

'When do you go to office?'

'What do you do on weekends?'

'How many friends do you have?'

'Do you have more male friends than females?'

Questions that were none of his business and yet she had to answer them because that was why she had been brought there: to answer whatever the boy's family asked. As time passed, Rivanah became increasingly bored and, as a result, started yawning more and more, to a point when it became embarrassing.

'Do you want to sleep for a bit, Mini?' Mr Dutta asked.

Rivanah glanced at her parents once and then at Mr Dutta.

'No, uncle, it is just that I haven't slept well for the last few days, with all the travelling.'

'Totally understandable. Youngsters these days have a mad schedule indeed,' Mr Dutta sympathized.

'Why don't you take a short nap? You'll look fresh by the time Mr Dutta's family gets back,' Mr Bannerjee chipped in.

Look fresh in front of Mr Dutta's son, that's the whole point, Rivanah thought.

'We will wake you up the moment Rishabh and his mother arrive.'

Rivanah gestured to her mother to come along for a second. 'Bhola, show madam the bedroom,' Mr Dutta said aloud.

The servant immediately appeared from the kitchen and escorted both Rivanah and Mrs Bannerjee to the master bedroom.

'Isn't it odd to sleep like this at someone else's place?' Rivanah said, keeping her voice in check.

'And what was it that you were doing sitting there? Yawning away like anything.' Her mother sounded cross.

'I'm sorry but I couldn't help it. I'm feeling very sleepy.'

'Then just sleep. I will wake you up when his son and wife come,' she said and walked out of the room. Rivanah sighed with yet another wide-mouthed yawn. She sat down on the bed. A moment later she lay down closing her eyes, telling herself she will not sleep. But she dozed off as soon as her head hit the pillow. When Rivanah woke up, she wondered why the interior of the room was so familiar. And then it hit her—she was lying in her own bedroom.

2

'Mumma!' Rivanah screamed as she sat upright with a jolt. Her mother came running, looking worried.

'What happened, Mini?' she asked.

'How did I come to my room? And did Mr Dutta's son and wife ever come?'

'What are you talking about, Mini?' her mother asked, looking aghast. 'You came back from your friend's place, had lunch and slept like a log.'

'Like a log? How many hours has it been?' Rivanah got off her bed and picked up her mobile phone from her study table.

'It is 9.30 p.m.!' she said aloud.

'I thought you were tired so I didn't wake you up,' her mother said and then, turning back, added, 'Come along now. Dinner is almost ready.'

'Mumma, tell me you are kidding.' Rivanah stopped her mother.

'Kidding about what, Mini?'

'You, Baba and I had gone to Mr Dutta's place for lunch today, right? I was feeling sleepy, so I went to his bedroom to sleep. What happened after that?'

Her mother's worried look was back.

'What are you talking about, Mini? Are you all right?' Rivanah looked hassled as she left her mother in the room and rushed to her father downstairs. He was sitting at the dining table waiting for dinner to be served. He was holding a copy of Tagore's *Gitanjali*. He dog-eared the page he was reading and looked up to see his daughter standing right in front of him.

'Tell your mother I'm very hungry,' he said.

'Baba, didn't we go to Mr Dutta's house today for lunch?'

Mr Bannerjee looked at her for a moment. Then, removing his specs, he said, 'We were supposed to but he had some work, so we didn't go. Why, what happened?'

Rivanah's jaws dropped.

'I don't know what she is talking about,' Mrs Bannerjee joined them.

'What is she saying?' Mr Bannerjee looked at his wife.

'That we went to Mr Dutta's place and she felt sleepy and . . .'

'Did you have a nightmare, Mini?' Mr Bannerjee asked Rivanah, cutting his wife short.

Rivanah, for a trice, seemed lost. Then she nodded. *Was it all a dream? Her coming home, going to Esplanade metro station with her mother and then being picked up by her father, going to Mr Dutta's house, him saying his wife and son are out.* Rivanah immediately called Ishita.

The number you have called is not reachable right now.

She checked her call log and found a call from her mother during the day.

'See, you called me in the morning,' she said, showing the phone to her mother.

'Of course, I did. I called and asked you to come over because we had to go to Mr Dutta's house. But the meeting was cancelled by the time you came home. Then you slept until you woke up a few minutes back,' her mother said, with a surety even Rivanah couldn't question.

A frustrated Rivanah sat with a thud in the chair right opposite her father.

'You should eat properly,' her mother said and moved towards the kitchen to serve them dinner. Rivanah didn't notice Mr and Mrs Bannerjee exchanging a furtive glance.

'This is what is wrong with your generation,' Mr Bannerjee started, 'You think money is everything and compromise on your health in the process. All this forgetfulness happens when you eat junk all day. These American food joints are spoiling our kids and their future, I tell you.'

Rivanah pushed her chair back and got up to leave.

'Mini?' Mr Bannerjee sounded worried.

Rivanah went straight to her room and opened her wardrobe to look for the salwar suit she had worn to Mr Dutta's place. She remembered it distinctly. *It couldn't possibly be a dream*, she thought, furiously ruffling through her wardrobe but she didn't find what she was looking for. Disappointed, she turned around to see her mother standing by the door.

'Can you tell me what's wrong with you?' Mrs Bannerjee asked.

'Mumma, where's that salwar suit that we bought the last time I was here?'

'Which one?'

'The peacock-green one with the red border.' Rivanah could have easily referred to it as the one she wore to Mr Dutta's place but she didn't.

'Oh that! It's in my wardrobe.'

Rivanah glared at her mother. 'What is my dress doing in your wardrobe, Mumma?'

'I had given it to be washed and kept it all ironed after you left. Forgot to put it back.'

Rivanah wasn't convinced.

'Show me,' Rivanah said and walked out of her room. Her mother followed.

Her mother opened the wardrobe in the master bedroom and there in one of the shelves lay her neatly ironed dress. 'Now do you believe me?' Mrs Bannerjee said, sounding hurt. Rivanah nodded and after thinking for a moment muttered under her breath, 'I'm sorry, Mumma. Let's have dinner. Baba is waiting.' *Maybe I am turning paranoid*, Rivanah thought.

All through dinner, her parents kept talking but Rivanah wasn't listening. She tried Ishita's number a couple of times but each time the automated voice told her the phone was not reachable. After dinner Rivanah checked her phone again. There were two missed calls from Danny and one message from Ekansh. Rivanah read the message first.

Hi, what's up?

The time of the message was 4.46 p.m. She checked the time of Danny's calls: 3.30 p.m. and 7.58 p.m. Rivanah immediately called Danny. He picked up on the fourth ring.

'Hey baby, where are you?'

'Hi! I'm sorry, Danny. I just dozed off in the afternoon.' Rivanah decided against recounting to him the confusing events of the day.

'You didn't send me your convocation pictures. How was the event?'

Images of her, along with Ishita, following her colleague Argho to her deceased college-mate Hiya's house flashed before her eyes.

'Hello?' Danny was waiting for her response.

'Oh, sorry. The event was great. I have few pictures on Ishita's phone. I shall ask her to share them with me. I will WhatsApp you.'

'Ishita?' Danny sounded clueless.

'The girl because of whom we met,' Rivanah said and remembered how Ishita had told her about this hot guy who had swept her off her feet at first sight. How they had had a bet to woo this guy. And that hot guy was now her boyfriend. Certain memories take your soul out for a sunbath. Her meeting Danny for the first time wrapped in only a towel was one such memory.

'Oh! Now I remember. Your old roomie?'

'Right. She is working here in Kolkata now.'

'That's good. And when are you coming back? I miss you.'

A smile featured on Rivanah's face. Nothing can beat the feeling of being desired by someone. 'I miss you too. Just a couple of days more and I'll be there.'

'Now that will give me a good night's sleep.' He kissed her over the phone. She kissed him back. After the Nitya incident, when Rivanah had wrongly doubted his loyalty, Danny had suddenly become this close-to-perfect boyfriend. Which girl would not desire someone who is hot, caring and gives ample space to you to the extent that even if he had an inkling that you were in touch with your ex, he still doesn't ask you awkward questions. But the other important question was: was she a close-to-perfect girlfriend to him? Rivanah was yet to confess to Danny about what had happened in the flat between Ekansh and her—that they had made love as if nothing had ever gone wrong between them. And it was scary because this feeling was like a seed which could proliferate into a gigantic tree with innumerable forbidden branches sprouting fresh leaves of illicit desires.

'Hello? You there?'

'Yes, yes. I'm here.' Rivanah came out of her momentary trance.

'I said I love you.'

'I love you too, Danny,' she said and cut the line. She sat on her bed lost in thoughts when her phone buzzed with a WhatsApp message.

How are you? No response?

It was Ekansh again. He was online. So was she now. Rivanah replied.

I'm good. How are you? And Tista?

She sent it and fixed her eyes below Ekansh's name on WhatsApp where it was written: *online*. Then it changed to *typing . . .* and then *online* again. A response came:

Can we please meet?

Sure. Tomorrow around noon?

Now?

Now? It's past 10! Mumma and Baba won't allow it.

Like old times?

He shouldn't have used those words: old times. Not now, not ever. She knew what he meant though. It wasn't the first time Ekansh wanted to meet her at a time when moving out of her house was next to impossible. Back when they were in college and in a relationship, she would sneak out of the house after her parents had slept. Rivanah typed out a four-letter word and pressed Send. Her message read: *Okay.*

3

Rivanah waited until her parents were done watching their favourite Bengali soap and retired to bed. When her mother came to leave a bottle of water in the room, Rivanah feigned drowsiness and wished her goodnight. Once her mother left, switching the lights off, Rivanah waited for some more time before sneaking out. This was such a familiar routine. The fact that she was still good at it told her how invested she had been in what Ekansh and she had called a 'relationship'. And love. Does love end when a relationship ends? Or does a relationship end because love has ended? And what were Ekansh and Rivanah into now? She didn't dare name it. But was this too because of what they had been earlier? Isn't the aftermath of love also . . . *love*?

Her mind still full of such thoughts, Rivanah took the keys out from under the old shoe rack beside the terrace door, unlocked the door and closed it gently behind her. Theirs was a two-storeyed house, so the terrace wasn't at a huge height. All she had to do was jump from the cemented parapet; Ekansh would catch her. She felt an awkwardness clinch her muscles. It is one thing to write 'like old times' in a message but it wasn't old times. They weren't a couple any more.

'Jump,' Ekansh said softly. Rivanah nodded and jumped as he caught her in his arms. He held her the way he used to and yet it felt different. She quickly severed herself from any kind of bodily touch from him. They quietly walked to Master da's tea stall where boys from the locality were playing carom while gossiping and drinking lemon tea. As they neared the stall, Rivanah stopped. What if the boys told on her? She would become the talk of the town by the next morning. How had she dared to do such things before? And why was she fighting it now? Was it because she really felt Ekansh and she shouldn't be seen together or because she didn't want those 'old times' to replay?

'Let's not go there,' she said. Ekansh gave her a look of understanding and took a lane leading to a small park. She followed. Sitting on a lonely bench in the park, the distance between them was palpable. Rivanah could almost see their past selves on a bench on the other part of the park. But unlike their present, their past selves' hands were clasped together.

'Why are we here, Ekansh?' Rivanah asked abruptly.

'Tista's surgery is tomorrow.' There was a forlorn look on Ekansh's face. As if he already knew what was going to happen inside the operation theatre the next day.

'But you told me earlier there's a 30 per cent chance of survival. I'm sure she will make it,' she said.

'What if Tista dies, Rivanah? Will you marry me?' Ekansh blurted. Rivanah couldn't help but give him a shocked look.

'I'm sorry. I don't mean it the way it sounds.'

'Then what did you mean, Ekansh?'

'I haven't slept since we both came back to Kolkata.'

Rivanah could tell he was telling the truth by the look in his eyes—tired, withdrawn and somewhat lifeless. She had noticed it when she met him that night in her flat in Mumbai but she didn't say anything lest he interpreted as concern. Though Rivanah had deliberately chosen to meet Ekansh at this hour, she didn't want him to read too much into it.

'All I keep thinking about is what will happen if Tista doesn't survive the surgery,' Ekansh said.

'Have you been really thinking that, Ekansh?'

'Yes.'

'No.'

'What do you mean no?'

'You have been thinking of what will happen to *you* if Tista doesn't survive the surgery. And hence your question to me. You are simply being selfish.'

Ekansh sat back on the bench and looked at the night sky.

'This was always my problem, wasn't it? I was always selfish in love. When I was in love with you, and now when I'm in love with Tista.'

In the silence, Rivanah could hear a frog croaking somewhere close by, and at a distance she could again see their old selves laughing, her head on his shoulder. He used to love it when her hair fell on his face. Then Rivanah saw their old selves turn quiet suddenly. She remembered that, back then, every time they became quiet, they would end up speaking at the same time. 'Ekansh.' This time, it was only she who spoke. He didn't look at her.

'Tista will be all right. And then we will stop meeting like this,' she said.

Ekansh turned his head towards her quizzically.

'What?' she shrugged.

'Can't we . . . ?'

'No, we can't be friends any more,' Rivanah responded to his incomplete question.

'Tell me honestly, Rivanah—don't you want to be my friend?' By now Ekansh had turned around and was facing her.

She took her time to answer. 'No, I don't.'

'Then what are you doing here?' He didn't know why he held her hand while saying it. She didn't know why she didn't push it away. She slowly looked down and then drew her hand out of his grasp.

'I'm guilty of the same thing I'm accusing you of. I too am selfish,' she said, choking up.

'Aren't we all, in one way or the other?'

Maybe he is right, Rivanah wondered, but kept mum. She stood up and asked, 'What time is the surgery tomorrow?'

'They will take her in the OT around ten in the morning.'

'I'll try to see her before that,' Rivanah said, and walked away. She saw Ekansh's shadow stand up and follow her but she didn't turn back. While moving out of the park she noticed the old Rivanah and Ekansh breaking from a tight embrace and kissing passionately. She could feel a lump in her throat.

Ekansh helped Rivanah climb on to the cemented parapet and then left. Rivanah locked the terrace door, kept the keys under the shoe rack and went downstairs to her room. She opened the door noiselessly. Once inside her bedroom, she let out a long sigh. Ekansh's query echoed in her mind: *What if Tista doesn't survive the surgery tomorrow?* Her relationship with Danny won't be accepted by her parents anyway. Rivanah shook her head vigorously. *What the hell am I thinking?* She was about to lie down on her bed when the lights in her room came on. Before she could speak, she heard a man say, 'Where were you, Mini?'

Rivanah looked up and got the shock of her life.

4

'You scared me!' Rivanah exclaimed. For a moment, she had thought it was the stranger in her room. Her heart was still racing with fear. Her parents were standing by her wardrobe staring at her.

'Where did you go, Mini?' Mr Bannerjee repeated.

'I went outside.'

'How did you go? We checked the main door. It was locked from the inside.' Mrs Bannerjee sounded exasperated.

'Oh, Mumma, I meant I was in the terrace. Why would I go outside at this hour?'

'I checked the terrace,' Mr Bannerjee said. 'You were not there.'

'Of course I was there. Did you check the portion behind the water tank?' Rivanah was trying her best to sound confident. Mr and Mrs Bannerjee exchanged a thoughtful glance. 'The network wasn't holding up here, so I went there to talk to Ishita,' Rivanah lied. 'But why are you two so worked up about it?'

Mrs Bannerjee came to Rivanah, caressed her head and said, 'Nothing. We just panicked not seeing you in your room. That's all. Now sleep, Mini. You anyway keep working all the time in Mumbai.'

Rivanah, to make things look normal, kissed her mother and climbed back into bed.

'Goodnight, Baba. Goodnight, Mumma.'

'Goodnight.' Her father left the room. Her mother pulled a thin blanket over her, and, switching off the lights, followed her husband out. Rivanah finally relaxed. She had forgotten her phone in the room itself. When she checked it, she found there was only one new message. It was from Ekansh.

Thank you for being there.

The message had come a few minutes after she had come back into her house. Had she met him for his sake? Or was it because her own damaged self was seeking a repair through proximity to Ekansh? Would Ekansh really want to get back with her if Tista didn't survive the surgery? She immediately hated herself for having such a filthy thought. And then a filthier question occurred in her mind: Whom would she ultimately choose if given the option—Ekansh or Danny? On an impulse, Rivanah typed a response to Ekansh:

See you at the hospital tomorrow.

To Danny, she messaged: *I love you. Goodnight.*

After sending both messages, she switched off her phone to avoid any further communication with the world and shut her eyes tight. She dozed off after murmuring a short prayer for Tista's well-being.

Next morning, Rivanah reached the hospital around ten. Tista's entire family was there. So was Ekansh. He came towards Rivanah the moment he saw her.

'What happened?' she said, seeing everyone crowding outside the room.

'The nurse is dressing her up for the OT,' Ekansh said.

'Dressing?'

'They need to wear a different uniform for the OT.'

'Oh, okay,' Rivanah said, and went ahead to greet Tista's parents and a few relatives who had seen her the other time she had come to the hospital.

'Any idea how long the surgery will take?' she asked Ekansh.

'Two hours minimum—if there are no complications,' he said and brushed his hand against her. *Was it an accident?* Rivanah didn't know. She felt as if Ekansh wanted her to hold him. They exchanged a furtive glance and her presumptions were confirmed. Rivanah intentionally stood slightly away from him. The fact that he too took couple of steps back told her his guard was up as well. Rivanah saw two people walking towards them. They were Ekansh's parents and she knew them well. Especially his father who used to joke that Rivanah spared them the pain of finding a daughter-in-law for their good-for-nothing son. Rivanah touched their feet. They blessed her like old times, but it was very awkward. Before his parents could speak, Ekansh came forward and told them that Tista was Rivanah's friend as well. They gave them an unsure smile and went ahead to greet Tista's parents. Rivanah was itching to ask Ekansh what reason he had given his parents for their break-up. Had he told them the truth? Or had he fabricated a web of lies to keep his image intact?

A nurse emerged from Tista's room and asked, 'Who is Rivanah here?'

Everyone turned to look at Rivanah as if a judge had pronounced an unexpected death sentence.

'Tista wants to have a word with you before the operation,' the nurse said. Rivanah glanced at Ekansh who gestured her to go ahead. As she took a couple of steps towards the room, the nurse spoke up, 'Make it short. I have to take her into the OT in a minute.' The nurse waited outside while Rivanah, all eyes still on her, went inside Tista's room.

Once inside, Rivanah shut the door behind her. She saw Tista lying on the bed in a green hospital dress. The way she looked at Rivanah scared her. She looked like a doppelganger of the Tista she had met for the first time in her Mumbai flat.

'Hi, Tista,' Rivanah said with a forced smile and went to stand by the bed.

The response came after few seconds. 'Hi, Rivanah di.'

'All will be good. Don't worry.'

'Rivanah di, do you still love Ekansh?'

There was a momentary shock in Rivanah's eyes but she couldn't tell if she hid it well.

'Who told you . . . ?' Rivanah immediately realized her response shouldn't have started with those words.

'For how long?' Tista asked, looking blankly at Rivanah.

'We were together for four or five years before we broke up.'

'Did you guys break up because of me?'

'No! No, Tista. You came into the picture much later.'

For a few seconds, neither spoke, neither moved. Then Rivanah noticed a teardrop roll down Tista's cheek.

'When Ekansh came to our flat for the first time, did you guys . . . ?' Tista's voice trailed off. And the trailing voice brought back the memory of the evening Rivanah had locked deep in her conscious, labelling it as 'so what?' But now with Tista inquiring about it the label had changed into 'why'. Did Tista know what happened between her and Ekansh that evening? How could she unless Ekansh had told her about it? Or the . . . ?

'I will have to take her to the OT now,' the nurse interrupted. She was followed by two ward boys who entered the room with a stretcher. They picked Tista up and lay her on the stretcher. All the while, Tista's eyes were fixed on Rivanah. Even though Rivanah was seeking an accusation in Tista's eyes, she couldn't find any. And it made the guilt inside her churn her guts. She felt like throwing up.

As Tista was taken away, Rivanah too rushed out. She didn't stop for Ekansh. While he was busy with Tista, Rivanah took the elevator and went downstairs. She sat down on one of the seats in the waiting area and immediately broke down. A few people sitting beside her gave sympathetic glances, assuming some acquaintance of hers must be in a serious condition—not knowing it was her conscience on the ventilator.

Earlier she had to deal only with the fact that she couldn't tell Danny what had happened between Ekansh and her that evening, but now her guilt discovered a stepsister named shame. Rivanah buried her face in her lap as she sobbed and shuddered. Someone in the seat behind her was staring at her. If Rivanah had turned around and looked, the person would have caught her attention. But she didn't even lift her head. A few seconds later the person stood up and left. Rivanah was still sobbing when she heard someone say:

'The heart leads but the mind misleads, Mini.'

Rivanah's sobs paused instantly. In a flash, she turned around only to see a small recorder on the seat right behind her. She rubbed her eyes and stood up. She went to the row of seats behind her and picked up the recorder. She fast-forwarded it, rewound it but all there was in the recorder was a single sentence in a male voice.

The heart leads but the mind misleads, Mini.

She kept the recorder in her bag, knowing only too well who must have placed it on the seat. She was sure her chance to catch the person was long gone. Her phone flashed 'Ekansh calling' but she didn't answer the call. Feeling slightly dizzy, she went out, wary of the people around her, and took a cab home. She slept till evening. Once her parents left for a function, she went to take a shower. Sitting naked on the bathroom floor under the shower, she only had one thing on her lips—a prayer for Tista. Ekansh had called her again, but she didn't dare pick up the phone. The surgery must have ended but she didn't have the courage to find out how it went. If Tista had died, Rivanah would die of guilt. If Tista lived, she would perish in shame. She was about to burst into tears again when her eyes snapped open. The water from her shower was still cascading down her body. But Rivanah could smell something. She stood up in a flash and turned off the shower. *Something is surely burning*, she thought, quickly wrapping herself in the towel. She unlocked the bathroom door and was about to step out into her room when the sight in front of her shocked her. There was a bonfire in the middle of her room, with flames licking the ceiling. She could feel the heat and knew the fire would soon engulf her as well, and yet she couldn't move. Fear had clouded her instinct for survival.

The stranger is here to kill me. I'll die in no time. Just like Hiya Chowdhury, she thought. As the fire in the room grew,

Rivanah's eyes fell on one of the many windows in her room. It had a word written on it in red:

Your

She looked at the next window.

End

Then the next one:

Is

The fourth window:

Coming

And then the last:

Soon.

Rivanah collapsed on the floor.

5

Mr and Mrs Bannerjee had rushed home after a panic call from their neighbour. By the time they reached, there was already a small crowd gathered around the front door, along with a stationary fire engine with its siren on. The firemen informed Mr Bannerjee that everything was under control, they had arrived before the fire could do some real damage. When Mr and Mrs Bannerjee went inside, they found their daughter huddled up in a corner of her room.

'Someone was here, Mumma,' Rivanah said, bursting into tears.

While Mrs Bannerjee hugged and tried to console her, Mr Bannerjee called up the police who arrived within half an hour. By then Rivanah had come out of shock and was able to speak clearly.

'Do you have any idea how the fire started?' Police Inspector Rajat Das asked Rivanah. He was the younger brother of one of Mr Bannerjee's colleagues.

'I don't know. I was in the bathroom. I smelt something and came out to see my room engulfed in fire,' she recounted, with fear still lurking in her heart.

'Do you have enemies? Or did you fight with someone recently? Anything untoward?' Inspector Rajat urged on.

Rivanah was lost in thoughts.

'I'm asking because we have found some words on the window panes.'

'What words?' Mr Bannerjee was confused.

'It said: Your end is coming soon.'

Mr and Mrs Bannerjee exchanged a worried glance.

'Mini,' Mr Bannerjee said, 'are you hiding anything from us?'

Rivanah couldn't tell them about the Stranger. Who knew what he would do if she involved the police this time. Forget the Stranger, she had a few skeletons of her own to hide from her parents. She looked at her father and shook her head.

'Hmm.' Rajat stood from the chair.

'Don't worry,' he said, facing Mrs Bannerjee, 'We shall be quick with the investigation. I'll let you know if something comes up.' He turned to Mr Bannerjee and said, 'Do accompany us to lodge an FIR.'

'Certainly.' Mr Bannerjee followed Rajat to the door.

Rivanah was wondering whether she should tell the police about Argho. It was evident what his or the Stranger's intention was: to kill her. What if she didn't live long enough to tell them the name?

As Inspector Rajat took his leave, Rivanah blurted out, 'Argho has been following me.'

'Argho? Who is he?' Rajat came up to her once again. Her parents were behind him.

'He works with me in Mumbai.'

'You never told us about this guy Argho before!' Mr Bannerjee said.

'And why has he been following you?' Mrs Bannerjee was quick to ask.

'I don't know,' Rivanah said, feeling her mind go blank.

'There has to be some reason for taking his name?' Rajat asked.

Rivanah was in two minds. If she told the police that she thought Argho was the Stranger, then she would have to tell them the entire story. What if the Stranger killed her if she confessed? Rivanah swallowed a lump and said, 'I'm not sure. I saw him glancing at me in the office.'

'Just glancing at you? Hmm. Anyway, do you know where he lives in Mumbai?' Rajat asked.

Rivanah nodded.

'What's his full name?'

'Argho Chowdhury.'

'Did he follow you here to Kolkata?'

'Yes.'

'How are you sure?'

'He was there in the recently held convocation in my college a few days back.'

'Did he study with you in college?'

'No.'

'Then what was he doing in the convocation?'

Rivanah took her time before saying, 'I don't know.'

'Hmm. Any idea where he lives in Kolkata?'

Rivanah shot him an incredulous look and shook her head. For a second, she thought of giving the inspector the phone numbers of the Stranger she had stored, but knew it would be useless since he never used them under his name.

'Hmm, you said he works with you. So it won't be difficult to hunt him down and check if your suspicion is right.'

Inspector Rajat finally took his leave followed by Mr Bannerjee. Her mother stayed back with her.

'I don't know what we have done to anyone to deserve all this.'

'I'm not hurt, Mumma,' she said trying to emotionally shelter her mother. I'm not hurt *yet*, she said to herself.

'Can I please have some water? I'm very thirsty.'

'Yes. You should have some salt water, actually. You are perspiring a lot,' Mrs Bannerjee said and sauntered away. Mr Bannerjee came back and said, 'You should have told us about Argho before.'

'Baba, even I didn't know it would come to this. In fact, I don't have solid reason to suspect him. It's just that when the inspector asked if I have anyone in my mind, only his face came to me.'

'But why would he do such a fatal thing? Does he have a grudge against you?'

'I don't know, Baba. I'm sure if the police nab him he will confess whatever it is. If he is the guilty one, that is.'

'Did he do anything during or after the convocation?'

'Nothing.'

'Hmm.' Mr Bannerjee went away.

Rivanah picked up her phone and went to her Contacts. She had to talk to someone. She scrolled down till she stopped at a name: *Danny*. And right below it was *Ekansh*. Calling Danny would have been the right thing to do. But right things always had consequences. What if Danny sensed her unsettled tone and asked questions? Telling him one thing would invariably lead to telling him a lot of things, which she knew would complicate their relationship. Ekansh too could ask questions but with him she now had the luxury to dodge them. Rivanah tapped on Ekansh's name. She anyway had to inquire about Tista's surgery. She had already ignored it for too long. The phone was answered on the second ring but Ekansh didn't speak.

'Ekansh, you there?'

'Hmm.' He sounded grim.

'What happened? How was the surgery?' Rivanah said, feeling a tinge of guilt that she couldn't be there with him when the surgery happened.

'Tista hasn't gained consciousness as yet. She is under observation for twenty-four hours. I . . .'

Rivanah could sense he was crying.

'Where are you right now?'

'Home,' he said in a choked voice.

She knew he needed her. *Did Tista tell him that she knows?* The emotional desperation to be there for Ekansh made her uncomfortable. But a truth from within struck the bell of her conscience—Ekansh was more a part of her now, when they were separated, than when they were together. Whether she accepted this truth or not was a different story.

'Ekansh, I'm coming to your place,' she said in one breath and cut the line.

Though she tried to coax her father, he wouldn't let her leave the house on her own—not after what had happened. Rivanah had to lie that an urgent office work had come up, else she wouldn't have insisted. They reluctantly agreed. Mr Bannerjee dropped her at Ekansh's place. She didn't tell him it was his place to avoid unnecessary questions. Her father offered to wait outside but she promised to call him once she was done. After Mr Bannerjee drove away, she walked for half a kilometre and reached Ekansh's actual house. The lights were off. She pushed the gate open and noticed a faded board on it: Beware of dog. Ekansh used to have a bulldog named Engineer. It was a joke between Ekansh and her that engineers studied to become MNC dogs. Every time she entered through the gate, Engineer would come and wag his tail until she put him on her lap and let him lick her face. The dog had died the year they graduated but the board had remained intact. Ekansh probably never got a pet after that. She rang the doorbell, and Ekansh's mother answered the door. If she was surprised to see Rivanah, she didn't show it.

'Hello, aunty,' Rivanah blurted awkwardly.

'How are you, Rivanah?' Ekansh's mother usually called her Mini. *The way we address people tells us so much about our relationship with them*, she thought.

'I'm okay, aunty. Is Ekansh—?'

'He is in his room,' his mother answered before she could finish.

Rivanah walked in as she closed the door behind her. Sensing she wasn't very inclined to talk, Rivanah took the stairs to Ekansh's room. As she stood outside the door, she took a deep breath to negate the flashes from the past which were becoming clearer and clearer every second. This was the room in which they had secretly kissed so many times.

Rivanah knocked on the door.

'Mom, I told you to leave me alone.' Ekansh's pitch had an irksome tinge to it.

'It's me, Ekansh.'

Ekansh let her in and shut the door. Before she could say anything, he hugged her tightly, almost crushing her ribs. The way his hands gripped her back always aroused her before—and it was no different now.

'Ekansh . . .' she murmured. He half broke the hug and then tore away from her, probably sensing she was uncomfortable.

'Any news of Tista?' Rivanah asked quickly, not wanting to give time for memories to return. After all, Tista was the reason they were together in his room. Whatever they had between them was not supposed to be set on fire again. *Deep relationships probably never die*, she thought, *and always have the potential to be rekindled.*

'Not yet,' he said. 'Tell me she will be all right.'

Rivanah had never seen Ekansh behave like a kid. It just told her how much he loved Tista. During their relationship, she had never believed Ekansh could love anyone more than he loved her. But now, getting a glimpse of his love for Tista, she had mixed feelings. She wasn't sad about it. But she wasn't happy either.

'She will be all right.' Rivanah understood that Tista hadn't told Ekansh anything yet, or else that would have surely been his first question to her.

A few silent moments and a stare later, Ekansh added, 'Thanks for coming here. I needed you.'

Words like these from your ex can steal your peace, especially when the real you knows you aren't over him completely.

'I'm going to Mumbai the day after.'

Ekansh sat down beside the window without a word. He was staring at the floor. Rivanah could tell he was thinking hard.

'I know it is still early, but do you have any idea when Tista will be discharged?'

'Rivanah . . .' Ekansh raised his head and looked straight at her. It wasn't a normal look. It looked like something of uber importance had dawned on him and she was interrupting that realization. She had a hunch that whatever he was about to say could alter a lot of choices in her life. It made her heart beat faster.

'Just say it . . .' Rivanah said.

Ekansh shook his head and said, 'Nothing.'

There was most definitely something but why won't he say it? Rivanah wondered.

'You can be honest with me, Ekansh,' she said, feeling her throat go dry as she spoke.

'That's the problem. If we are always absolutely honest, we won't be able to live in peace.'

'Why do you say that?' Rivanah frowned slightly.

'It's because peace is an illusion created by either ignorance or acceptance.'

What are you trying to ignore, Ekansh? Or accept, for that matter? She desperately wanted to ask him but didn't, since she understood his point. She was oscillating between honesty and peace herself as far as her confession to Danny was concerned. Thinking about Danny, she wondered if she should tell Ekansh about her conversation with Tista. One look at Ekansh, however, and she knew he wouldn't be able to handle it.

'I'm not sure when I'll be in Mumbai,' he said.

'I get it. Let me know when you visit Tista next. I need to see her once.' *And apologize to her with all my heart,*

35

she said to herself, knowing full well a verbal apology would not be good enough to cleanse the dirt of guilt within her.

Rivanah's father came to pick her up from exactly where he had dropped her. Later in the night, when Rivanah joined her parents at the dining table, Mr Bannerjee gave her a bunch of papers.

'What's this, Baba?'

'One of Rajat's constables was here when you were out. It has the names of the passengers who travelled to Mumbai from Kolkata yesterday. The name you'd mentioned . . .'

'Argho Chowdhury,' Rivanah chipped in.

'Right. Argho's name is on the list, and the police have confirmed from the CCTV footage that he did go through the security check at the airport yesterday.'

He couldn't have set fire inside my bedroom, she thought.

'If he has flown back to Mumbai, then what am I to check in these papers?'

'These papers have the names of passengers who flew from Kolkata to Mumbai after the incident. The police want to know if you recognize any name.'

Rivanah kept flipping through the pages, going through each name with utmost focus. She paused on one name: Prateek Basotia.

6

Rivanah gave the papers back to her father saying, 'I don't know anyone from the list.' She had to first check if Prateek, her school senior and ex-colleague, was indeed the Stranger or not. But if he was, why would he call her to his place like he had done months back and then humiliate himself by recording his own self in a compromising manner only to help her out?

'What happened, Mini?' Mr Bannerjee asked.

'Nothing. I think I'll retire now. Goodnight, Baba, goodnight, Mumma,' said Rivanah, pushing her chair back. She got up and walked straight to her room.

Once inside, she opened Facebook and unblocked Prateek from her blocked list. She immediately went to his profile. His cover photo was of a woman's mehendi-adorned hands with a wrist full of red bangles. Her hand was holding a man's hand. The profile picture was of Prateek with a girl. A look at his About Me section confirmed her guess. His relationship status was 'Married to: Rati Agarwal Basotia'. Rivanah clicked on the hyperlink and Prateek's wife's profile opened. She appeared to be a typical Marwari girl with a domestic vibe. A casual glance at her timeline told Rivanah that she had checked-in at the Yellow Chilli restaurant in Bangur Avenue with Prateek Basotia at . . . Rivanah saw the time. It was about the same time the attack had taken place. Had Prateek paid someone to do it? He had all the reasons to be upset with her. Rivanah scrolled down Prateek's timeline. He had got married three months back. On a hunch she ran to her parents' room.

'Baba?' Rivanah said. The lights in the room were off. Both her parents woke up, startled.

'What happened, Mini?'

'Relax. I just wanted to check the passengers list once again,' she said, switching the lights on.

'It is right below that book,' Mr Bannerjee said pointing towards a table. Rivanah picked it up.

'Keep it with you tonight,' Mr Bannerjee said sleepily. Rivanah nodded and took the papers with her. She switched the lights off before leaving the room.

Back in her room, Rivanah opened the page which had Prateek's name on it. And right below was: Rati Agarwal Basotia. The two had clearly travelled together from Kolkata to Mumbai. Why would a guy who got married few months back take such a big risk of attacking a girl because of a grudge? What will he get out of it? It wasn't Argho if the police were to be believed, and now it was almost clear that Prateek's name was a coincidence. Then it could only mean the Stranger was still at large . . . unless . . . there were not one but several people involved. The thought itself made her heart skip a beat. What if there were not one but multiple Strangers? As Rivanah lay in bed, she kept wondering if she was missing out on any detail from the first day she had landed in Mumbai. An hour later, she fell asleep with a myriad of directionless thoughts.

Rivanah woke up late the next morning. She saw a few missed calls from both Ekansh and Danny. She called Danny while brushing her teeth and rushed through breakfast, still on the call, mostly listening to the latest news from his shoot. By the time she reached the hospital, it was around 10.30 a.m. The scene didn't look good. Tista's parents—especially her mother—were hysterical. Other relatives were trying to calm her down but in vain. She took a couple of steps towards them but nobody noticed her. She could see Ekansh's parents standing with Tista's relatives. With her heart beating harder, she went to the nurse who was writing something on a paper.

'What happened, sister?'

'The patient collapsed.'

'Collapsed?' Rivanah's throat had gone dry by then.

'Tista died early morning.'

Rivanah thought her heart had stopped for a moment. *Tista can't die. Tista shouldn't die. Tista hasn't died.* Tears started rolling down her cheeks. The nurse made a soft announcement that the body would be in the room for another half hour maximum.

Rivanah slowly turned towards the cabin door. It was a couple of metres away from her but she had to summon all her energy to be able to come up to it.

Standing by the door, she could see Ekansh sobbing beside Tista's bed. No medical equipment was attached to her body any more. Her eyes were shut. Rivanah wouldn't have guessed if she didn't already know. She still hoped Tista would miraculously open her eyes—and she would get a chance to apologize to her. At that instant, Rivanah knew nothing would give her more joy than seeing Tista and Ekansh together and happy. Tista's calm visage told her coming back to life was still possible while Ekansh's ashen face confirmed the improbability of it. Ekansh lifted his head when she entered the room. She had once believed Ekansh loved her truly and had changed her perception of him over the years, believing he could not be loyal to anyone. But he had surprised her with his behaviour towards Tista. A person can be good as well as bad, black and also white. Our experience of the person is only a way to perceive him or her. And perceptions come with inherent limitations, Rivanah now knew.

She placed a hand on Tista's forehead, caressing it. Ekansh grasped Rivanah's other hand. He tightened his grip; it hurt but she didn't move. Ekansh looked up at her and said, 'She knew.'

Those weren't just words but a pyre on which Ekansh's life would station itself. The fire of guilt shall

40

slowly lick his conscience all his life like it would lick hers. Till those words were spoken by him they had shared a past, but from now on, Ekansh and Rivanah would share the same fire of guilt in them. She wanted to talk to him but stopped herself when Ekansh's mother stepped into the room. Rivanah quickly managed to free her hand from his grasp. Ekansh's mother asked him to come out with her; he followed her out. Rivanah too left Tista's room but didn't see Ekansh or his parents.

Back from the hospital, Rivanah was too dazed to think clearly. She picked up her phone several times to call Ekansh but didn't know what they would talk about. At night, he messaged her saying he wanted to meet. Rivanah had just finished packing for her flight the next morning. She agreed and asked him to pick her up from her place. She convinced her parents that she was going to her friend's place like the other day for some office work and the friend would pick her up and drop her back as well.

'What is your friend's name and phone number?'

Rivanah gave them Ekansh's number but told them the name was Pooja, someone they knew.

Ekansh picked her up and they drove to the Kankurgachi footbridge. Neither uttered a word during the ride. Danny had called but Rivanah told him she was out with family and would call him back the moment she reached home. The two climbed the bridge and sat on the steps. The footbridge was a lonely place during the day. Even more so at night.

'Why did you tell her?' Ekansh asked.

'What?' Rivanah wasn't expecting this question.

'Why did you tell Tista what happened between us that evening?' Ekansh asked sternly.

I didn't, Rivanah thought. *Someone else did. But I can't tell you who that someone is.*

'Was this your revenge?'

'Revenge?'

'Because I ditched you.'

'You really think I'm capable of doing something so cheap, Ekansh? Like, really?'

'I don't know. How else did she come to know?'

'If you don't know, how would I know?' Rivanah raised her pitch a bit. It was frustration shielded as anger—frustration of not being able to tell Ekansh about the Stranger. She stood up, paced the bridge, came back calm and said, 'Maybe she just understood it. A girl's sense is very strong in these matters.'

'She understood it the day she died? You think I'm going to believe that?'

'What are you trying to say, Ekansh? Please be clear.'

'I said what I wanted to say. I know what I did to you wasn't good, but by telling Tista what happened between us that evening, you have scarred me for life.'

'I haven't scarred you for life, your own karma has.'

'What bullshit!' Ekansh stood up to face Rivanah.

'Bullshit? If I had told her about this, why would I not confess to you? I was always there whenever you needed me. Back then, when we were in a relationship, and now, when we aren't. But at both times you have shocked me with your behaviour.' The irritation was evident in her face. They could have done this over phone too if all Ekansh had in mind was blaming her unnecessarily.

'I know you were and are there for me, but that doesn't mean I'm going to believe you on this. There is no way a third person could have known what happened between us that evening in the flat. I know I didn't tell Tista anything. That leaves only one person who could have.'

Rivanah shot an angry glance at him.

'Do me a favour now. Please don't get in touch again,' Rivanah said and started stepping down the bridge's staircase. Ekansh caught up with her calling her name. 'Rivanah . . . listen, Rivanah.'

'There is nothing to listen. Be it love or friendship, if you can't trust the other person, there is no reason why you should be together,' she said.

'All right. Go. If you think that by putting the blame on a girl's sixth sense you would be able to absolve yourself, then you are mistaken. Just imagine me telling your boyfriend about what happened between us. Only then you will understand my pain.'

With that Ekansh had blown the lid off Rivanah's anger.

'It's a free world, Ekansh Tripathi,' she said, turning back. 'Do as you please.' She finally climbed down the footbridge stairs.

'Thank you for the suggestion,' Ekansh shouted behind her.

Rivanah didn't care to turn. She hailed a cab standing nearby and was on her way home. Her phone rang flashing Ishita's name. Rivanah wiped the tears from her eyes and took the call. 'Where were you, girl?' she asked.

'Sorry, I was at a remote place with my office team. Didn't have network coverage there. I just received a missed call alert. Did you find a lead to Hiya Chowdhury?'

'Now who on earth is Hiya Chowdhury? What are you talking about, Ishita?' Rivanah said. There was total silence from Ishita's side.

7

'Though I would have liked to go with you, Mini, I couldn't manage to get leave,' Mr Bannerjee said, kissing his daughter's forehead. Rivanah's parents were seeing her off at the airport.

'Don't worry, Baba. I can take care of myself. I'll be all right,' Rivanah said. Though her father's anxiety was to be expected, especially after the attack, this time he seemed more uncomfortable than last time she flew to Mumbai. She hugged him hoping it would help. So much had happened after the Stranger's attack that it didn't seem as threatening to her now as it had then.

'Take care, shona.' Mrs Bannerjee kissed her daughter's cheeks. And whispered in her ears, 'I have packed a box of nalen gurer sandesh for Danny. Baba doesn't know.' Rivanah couldn't help but kiss her mother back.

'I'll miss you both,' she said.

Right then one of the security personnel came up to Mr Bannerjee and asked him to move his car from the gate since he wasn't allowed to park there.

'You guys leave now. I'll call you right after my security check,' Rivanah said.

She waved her parents goodbye and waited till they drove out of sight. Then she walked briskly with her luggage to the departure gate nearby; Ishita was waiting for her there.

'Just tell me you were joking on the phone last night?' said Ishita the moment Rivanah reached her. Ishita couldn't make head or tail of what Rivanah was talking about when she had said she didn't know who Hiya Chowdhury was, so she had decided to meet her in person this morning.

'No, I wasn't. Who is Hiya Chowdhury? And why would I joke about someone whose name I'm hearing for the first time?' Rivanah was as genuine as she was on phone the previous night. Ishita showed her phone to Rivanah. There was a WhatsApp message Ishita had sent to Rivanah a couple of days before. It read:

I'm off for few days. Let me know if you come to know anything about Hiya.

Why isn't this message there in my phone when Ishita's WhatsApp shows a blue tick? Rivanah was clueless.

'I haven't read this message of yours,' Rivanah said aloud.

'Well, someone did.'

Was it the Stranger? Rivanah wondered. Ishita took a few minutes to relay all that Rivanah had told her regarding the Stranger and Hiya after she reached Kolkata. She also recounted how they had followed Argho to Hiya's house, met her parents and realized Rivanah's life could be in danger since they both believed the Stranger might have killed Hiya.

I remember the Stranger, Rivanah wondered, *I also remember Argho but why don't I remember Hiya Chowdhury and the visit to her house then? Ishita can't be lying about this girl named Hiya. Why would she?*

'Now don't tell me you have forgotten it all?' Ishita looked a little unnerved.

Rivanah nodded. 'I really don't remember any of this.'

'Oh my God. Does the Stranger practise some black magic shit?'

Rivanah swallowed a lump remembering the fire in her room. *Your end is coming soon.* Was the Stranger really going to kill her? But why? What harm had she done to him? On the contrary, she had always done whatever he had asked of her—except, she hadn't confessed to Danny yet. The Stranger had already avenged that by telling Tista about it. What more did he want?

'I think you should go now,' Ishita said, looking at the board. It was time for security check.

'Yeah, I suppose I should.'

'But I'm really worried for you, dear. Just take care and let me know if I can help. If something out of the ordinary happens, do inform Uncle and Aunty,' Ishita instructed, hugging her friend. Once she broke the hug, Rivanah pulled her luggage and went inside. She went straight to the security check and realized she hadn't collected her boarding pass. She could sense a tension brewing within her and it made her head reel. She sat down for a moment holding her head. Nothing was making sense. If Ishita was to be believed, she already knew a lot about Hiya, so then why could she not remember anything? Just then her phone rang. It was her father.

'We just reached home. Are you done with your security check, Mini?'

'Yes, Baba. All done,' she somehow managed to speak.

'Good. Call me once you board,' he said and hung up.

Rivanah knew she couldn't sit there for long. She went to collect her boarding pass. Right after the security check, she saw Danny's missed call on her phone. Only she knew how much she craved to be in his strong arms that moment, safe and sound. She immediately called him back.

'Hey baby.' He answered on the first ring.

'I love you, Danny.'

'Whoa, I'm having a morning wood and your voice isn't helping much.'

Rivanah managed a smile. 'Just hold it. I'll be there in three hours.'

'I'm not a fucking Viagra that I will hold-on for that long without you here. So give me enough reason to prolong my hard on,' Danny said naughtily.

He didn't know she wasn't quite in the mood.

'Actually Danny . . .'

'Airports have washrooms, right?'

He is really in the mood now, Rivanah thought, and decided it would be better to tell him about what was troubling her when they met.

'Hold on, cowboy,' she said and cut the line. Rivanah located the ladies' washroom, went straight inside the toilet and shut the door. She quickly raised her top to expose her royal-blue bra and clicked a pouting selfie showcasing her soft cleavage. She sent the picture to Danny.

That's such a lifesaver. Thanks, baby. Have a safe flight back. Your cowboy is waiting. In fact, both your cowboys are waiting. He WhatsApped back with a wink emoticon.

She replied with three kiss emoticons. And then sat on the toilet sink trying to think clearly. *Why the hell can't I remember Hiya Chowdhury? Who deleted Ishita's message from my phone?* Nothing made sense; she gave up. Rivanah slept through the entire flight.

By the time she reached her flat in Lokhandwala, Andheri West, she had prepared herself to meet Danny with as much eagerness as he had voiced on phone few hours back. She noticed the door was already slightly ajar. With a frown she pushed the door open and was taken aback. The entire room was stuffed with heart-shaped balloons. There were so many that she couldn't even step inside. She caught hold of a balloon and read what was written right across the centre: *Will you marry me?*

She checked two more balloons, and they all had the same thing written on them. A smile touched her face. This was completely unexpected.

She called out to Danny. 'Baby, you there? How do I come in?'

'If your answer is yes,' Danny said from somewhere inside the flat, 'take the lighter kept under the doormat and burst the balloons to come in.'

She picked up the lighter, and burst the first balloon. Then she burst another one, and another one. She managed to squeeze into the flat and close the main door behind her.

'Keep coming,' Danny said.

With a smile, Rivanah punctured another one with the lighter. Slowly it turned into a game she was starting to enjoy. The more balloons she burst, the deeper she went into her own flat. Finally she saw Danny right in the middle of the room, where he had positioned himself amidst the balloons.

'How did you do that?' she said, checking him out. He was in his boxer shorts. Only his boxer shorts.

'Do you think I'm in the mood to talk?' Danny said and lifted her. He took her to the bedroom where he had sprinkled rose petals all over the bed.

'I must say I'm impressed,' she said as Danny placed her on the bed.

'Now time to impress me,' he said and tugged down his boxers. He was kneeling on the bed while Rivanah was lying on her back looking at him. Her eyes slowly went down to his raging hard-on. She moistened her dry lips with the tip of her tongue. After the weeks-long dry spell, a sexual monsoon loomed large as Rivanah pushed him on the bed with her feet. She then sat on top of him, putting both her legs on either side. In a flash, she removed her tee. As she bent down to kiss him, he unhooked her bra. It came off as she sat straight again. She was getting aroused slowly. She started rubbing her pelvis on his hard-on, turning it even harder. He unbuttoned her jeans, unzipped it and, with her help, tugged it down along with her panties. He was surprised how wet she was. As he held his penis, she lifted her back only to sit on it gently, allowing it to quite deftly go inside her. With her hands on his chest, Rivanah shut her eyes tight and started slowly moving her pelvis. As the initial pain of insertion slowly turned into pleasure, her mind kept switching between pleasure and reality. Though she didn't like how things had ended with Ekansh, she now felt it was for the best. With Ekansh in her life, she had to constantly juggle between whether to tell Danny the truth or not, but now when she was sure of not seeing Ekansh's face ever again, she could well bury the sexual slip in her subconscious labelling it as 'a nothing'.

Danny flipped her without warning, and from her being on top, it changed into the missionary position.

Danny took her legs on his shoulders, rubbing his face on her calf, while Rivanah still had her eyes shut, clutching the bed sheet tight with both hands. His intense and strong thrusts felt like he was making her disappear. With every passing moment, she felt as light as a feather. All her defences seemed conquered, all her filters seemed compromised. If Danny had probed at that moment she would have confessed what had happened between Ekansh and her in the flat. Feeling his breath on her face, she opened her eyes. Danny had leaned forward and was now close to her. His lips pursed hers, and in no time, he took her tongue in his mouth. She understood that confession was the easy part. What was difficult was the explanation. Why were she and Ekansh intimate in the flat even though they had broken up long before that? Until that moment, she had sworn to herself she hated Ekansh up to the hilt. How could she dress the complex thoughts that propelled her to first indulge in the act with all her heart and then keep it a secret from Danny with words? *How does one explain the plausibility of such a thing?* Rivanah wondered, as she felt Danny squeezing her boobs with both his hands and sucking on her nipples alternately. He had increased his pace by now and she had wrapped her legs tightly around him to escalate her pleasure. Soon the thrusts became even harder, the moans louder, and they both climaxed as Danny came inside her. Both were panting as he looked at her and said, 'Sorry, I came inside you.'

'It's okay. I'm on my safe period. Hopefully!' she winked at him. He kissed her. Danny flipped her once again, bringing her on top of him. She placed her ears on his chest and could hear his heart beat fast. He held her tight in his arms. They slept in that position for a good five hours. When she woke up with a start, it was close to lunchtime. The fact that she should have been at work made her sit up. But right then, a strong pull made her collapse on the bed again.

'No office today,' Danny said in a groggy tone.

'Why?'

'Because I said so. One more day of leave won't change anything.'

Rivanah looked at him and caressed his already ruffled hair. To her, he seemed like the most desirable man on the planet. She picked up her phone and texted her teammate to manage without her for one more day. Next, she called her parents and told them she had reached Mumbai safely and would have called sooner had she not slept. The moment she put the phone down, Danny pulled her towards him and pinned her hands to take control of her.

'Relax. I'm not going anywhere,' she said, with a warm smile.

'Yes, you are,' Danny said.

'Huh?'

'To fairyland.'

Before she knew it, Danny was kissing his way to her navel. She somehow managed to push him away saying, 'Let's eat something first.' She climbed down and took out a pair of shorts and a spaghetti top from her wardrobe. She could sense Danny's eyes on her all the time. It made her blush. As Rivanah went to the kitchen to fix a meal, Danny came from behind and scooped her up, lifting her off the kitchen floor.

'Danny!'

Before she could say anything, he took her to the bathroom and placed her under the shower. As the water came cascading down, she knew how much he had missed her. And with every kiss, she realized how much she too had missed him.

'I want to eat her first,' he said. She knew what he meant as he went down on his knees, putting the tip of his tongue on her belly button. Rivanah gripped his hair tightly. He had always been passionate in his lovemaking. The pleasure hormones released by Danny's touch made her feel lucky, accepted, wanted and thoroughly desired. Danny stood up. As they smooched under the cold shower, she realized whatever had happened was for good. Now she won't have to fight guilt. Ekansh was finally history and so was whatever had transpired between them.

After a prolonged fondling under the shower, they finally had lunch. Having catered to the two most basic requirements of human beings—sex and food, they collapsed on the bed. Rivanah and Danny slept in a tight embrace, as if never wanting to let go. Listening to Danny's soft snores, she too closed her eyes.

Rivanah woke up startled and anxious. She had had a nightmare . . . *someone was following her . . . she was running in a forest . . . all alone . . . discovering a wooden house . . . and then seeing herself in a sexual act with a man whose face was hidden . . . and as he tried to press her throat and kill her* . . . Rivanah relaxed when she realized she was lying beside Danny. It had been some time since she had had a nightmare. In the silence of the room, she could hear her heart beating fast. Danny shifted slightly asking her if there was any problem. She said no and asked him to go back to sleep, got down from the bed to fetch some water when she heard a bell ring a couple of times. She went to the window and saw an ice-cream wallah who had brought his small van inside their building Krishna Towers for eager children. An intense desire for ice cream propelled her to leave Danny alone in the flat and rush out to get one.

As she was coming back after buying an ice cream for herself, just when she was about to step into her wing, someone threw a bucket full of water on her—or so she thought. Looking up towards the terrace, she hurled an abuse at whoever it was. But she stopped dead when a staunch smell of kerosene infiltrated her nostrils. She had been drenched in kerosene! And when she looked up again, she saw a flaming arrow approaching her. She knew she had to move away or else . . .

8

The arrow fell right beside Rivanah's feet. The ground where the kerosene had spilt caught fire immediately. Survival instinct pushed Rivanah to dash towards the building entrance. The fire trailed her rapidly. It was about to touch her when one of the two security guards seated at the entrance came and poured an entire bottle of water on it, extinguishing the trail. The guard looked up at Rivanah who was screaming her lungs out. He tried to calm her down but her screams only escalated. A few residents of the colony peeped out of their windows. Rivanah stopped her screams and said, 'He will kill me.'

'Take her to her flat,' one of the inhabitants shouted at the guard from the first-floor flat.

'Is there someone living with her?' asked another.

'Call the police maybe,' said a third.

A woman who lived on the ground floor took Rivanah to the elevator with the help of one of the guards and then to her flat, while the other guard went to the terrace and the other flats to try and find out who could be behind all this.

Danny was shocked to see Rivanah shuddering when he opened the main door all confused. She hugged him tightly. The guard felt awkward and, without clarifying, left the couple and went up to the terrace to join his colleague. Danny closed the door behind.

'What happened, baby? When did you go out? And why are you smelling of . . .' Danny sniffed and added, 'kerosene?'

'He tried to kill me.'

'*He?*' Danny's heart skipped a beat. 'Who is this *he?*'

'Argho Chowdhury.'

'Who is this guy?' Danny said, cupping her face and compelling her to make an eye contact.

'He works in my office.' *And I am sure he is the Stranger.* But she couldn't tell Danny that.

'Why the hell would he try to kill you? Are you hiding anything from me, Rivanah?' Danny's eyes showed evidence of genuine care. And what she had for him was a lie.

'No.'

A guilt-laden no. That's all she could manage before averting her eyes.

'Then is he a lunatic to try to kill you?'

Rivanah looked up at him and said softly, 'I'm scared, Danny.'

He hugged her tighter.

'You don't have to be as long as I'm with you,' he whispered in her ears. 'First, take a shower and get rid of this smell.'

57

Danny guided her to the shower and closed the bathroom door. Rivanah took off her clothes and stood under the shower. The image of the fireball flashed in front of her eyes. What if she had not seen it coming? She would have had burnt to death by now. She slowly applied the shower gel to get rid of the kerosene smell, all the while trying to get a grip on herself. *Why the hell does Argho want to kill me? Revenge? For what? Have I forgotten something the way I forgot about Hiya Chowdhury a few days back? Am I suffering from amnesia or Alzheimer's?*

Rivanah came out of the shower after almost an hour. She was feeling and smelling fresh. Danny was working on his laptop.

'How are you feeling now?' he asked.

'Better.' She came to him and kissed him on the cheeks.

'For you,' he said as he pushed a mug with steaming black coffee towards her.

'Thanks.'

'The guards told me they didn't notice anyone or anything odd in the terrace.'

I was sure they didn't, Rivanah thought.

'Now tell me what you haven't told me yet,' Danny said.

Rivanah's heart skipped a beat.

'Who is Argho?' he said.

Rivanah swallowed a lump and then spoke, 'I think he is the Stranger.'

There was a deep frown on Danny's face.

'You mean . . .'

Rivanah nodded as if she had read his mind.

'Why didn't you tell me before?' He sounded cross.

'I never thought it would come to this.'

'That's not the point. The point is that you didn't tell me about it.'

'I'm . . . sorry . . . Danny.' Only she knew she was apologizing for more than one thing.

In the silence that followed, they stood hugging each other with Danny caressing her back.

'I was just talking to a friend. He said he has good connections with the police.'

'Hmm,' Rivanah said, feeling Danny break the hug. As they settled on the bed, Rivanah picked up her phone. *Should I message the Stranger and ask him what the fuck he wants from me?* She scrolled down her Contacts. It had been some time since she had had any sort of communication with him. But was there any point in messaging him? He had made his intention clear: he wants her dead—for reasons best known to him. If Ishita was to be believed, they had together guessed that the Stranger may have killed Hiya as well and projected the entire incident as a suicide and was now pinning it all on Rivanah. *But . . . why?* She heard Danny's phone buzz.

'My friend messaged saying he will take us to his uncle who is the assistant commissioner of Mumbai,' Danny said.

'Thanks, Danny,' Rivanah said. It was time something was done about the Stranger.

9

Rivanah was the first to wake up the next morning. Giving a peck to a sleeping Danny, she went to fetch the milk packets and the day's newspaper from her doorstep. As she crossed the living room to reach the kitchen, she noticed a sketch board. She frowned; she hadn't noticed it lying there before. She tossed the newspaper on the sofa and sauntered to the kitchen to put the milk packets in the fridge and then came right back to stand in front of the board. There was a sketch of a pair of eyes, a nose, lips and ears but the contour of the face was missing. *Danny never told me he sketches*, she wondered and checked the sketches under the first one. Each of them had her name signed at the bottom-right corner. She was about to turn around when she felt a pair of hands around her waist.

'What are you doing, baby?' It was Danny.

'Did I sketch these?'

'Of course, you did,' Danny said and licked the back of her ears subtly. It tickled her senses but her mind was elsewhere. If she had sketched them, why didn't she remember it? Just like she didn't remember Hiya Chowdhury? Why did Ishita have to relay everything she had experienced herself only days back? Rivanah was deeply immersed in her thoughts.

'What happened?' Danny said, sensing a certain stiffness in her.

'Nothing.'

'Not in the mood?'

She gave him a weak smile.

'I understand. Anyway, get ready,' he said, giving her a peck on the cheek. 'We need to go to the police first. Then I have to meet the producer of my film.'

'How is the film going, Danny?' Rivanah said and felt a tad guilty for not having asked sooner. She had been so preoccupied with what was happening in her own life that she had forgotten that Danny's life too, somewhere, touched her. The last time she had inquired about him was when she had talked to him on phone from Kolkata.

'So far so good. Two more shoot schedules left. One in Mumbai and the other one in Delhi.'

'Great. By the way, I have to go to office today. I can't take any more leaves.'

'That's why I said, get ready quickly.'

Danny and Rivanah picked up his friend from Bandra, and together they went to the friend's uncle's place in Mumbai Central. All through the drive, Rivanah kept quiet but her mind was constantly probing the reason for her forgetfulness. First Hiya, and now the sketches. This, she understood, had to be the second dot—forgetting Hiya was the first. But she had never forgotten the Stranger. Were these two dots exclusive of the Stranger? Or, would she get the third dot only when she joins the first two properly? Every question was a dead end and it made her all the more frustrated. Moreover, now she only knew as much about Hiya Chowdhury as Ishita had relayed to her. What about the stuff she may have known earlier? How the hell had she become so forgetful?

Danny's friend took them to his uncle, Assistant Commissioner Dharmesh Waghdhare, whose house had a constant influx of constables. At fifty-five, Mr Waghdhare had a rather amicable personality for a police officer. He met the trio over breakfast. It was Danny who narrated what had happened the previous night.

'So nobody has seen the person who threw kerosene on her?'

'No. I asked the security guards and other people this morning, but nobody saw any one,' Danny said.

'Aren't there any CCTV cameras in your building?'

'No, sir.'

'Do you suspect anyone?'

Rivanah glanced at Danny and then said, 'There is a senior in my office.'

'Argho Chowdhury,' Danny added.

'And why would he do such a thing? Spurned lover, you think?' Dharmesh asked, finishing his poha and taking a sip from his mango shake.

'I never got any love-struck vibes from him, which is why I'm all the more confused—why would he do something like this?' Rivanah wondered aloud, fully aware that she wasn't making much sense. She wanted to disclose the Kolkata incident to Waghdhare and that a complaint had already been registered with the Kolkata Police, but, because of Danny's presence, she didn't. She had still not told him about it and disclosing it now would only put a strain on his trust. According to the Kolkata Police, Argho had an alibi. He flew out of Kolkata a day before the incident. But he could have bribed someone else to come to her house and create the deadly mess.

'Hmm, you don't seem to know of any possible reason, but you still think Argho could be trying to kill you? That's a big allegation,' he said. Waghdhare had years of experience which had sharpened his instinct for crime. He felt Rivanah was hiding something. Or that some important part of the puzzle was missing.

'The thing is, I can get this Argho guy picked up for interrogation, but I would rather catch him red-handed. If he is guilty, that is.' He looked at all of them one by one as he spoke. 'So I'll ask one of my men to follow him for a week or so. Let's see what comes up.'

'What if he attacks again?' Rivanah blurted.

'My man will be there. Any suspicious activity, and Argho Chowdhury will be taken into custody.'

Rivanah moistened her dry lips anxiously and glanced at Danny. 'So we will leave now, uncle,' his friend said, as he stood up.

'Sure,' Dharmesh said and turned to Rivanah to say, 'My man will contact you in some time. Give him all the details of Argho Chowdhury, and when you are in office, make sure you don't make it obvious that he's a suspect. Also, remain alert always.'

'Sure, sir,' Rivanah said, and left with Danny who dropped her to her office. Once Rivanah was in, she was extra conscious of Argho's presence. Though their cubicles were far apart, if she pushed her chair back a little, Argho's cubicle would be visible to her.

Argho came in half an hour late. The promised phone call from the policeman came within minutes of Argho's arrival in the office. Rivanah told him whatever she could about Argho. The policeman, Sadhu Ram, asked her to calm down and to make sure her suspicion wasn't obvious. The rest he would manage since he had already collected Argho's photograph, address and phone number. Though Rivanah had piles of work, she kept her eyes on Argho. If he went to the washroom, she excused herself and paced up and down right in front of the men's washroom. She was sure Argho would message her from inside the washroom from one of the Stranger's numbers. But nothing happened. Instead, there was a momentary, awkward eye contact with Argho when he came out of the washroom.

'Hey, congrats,' he said.

'Huh?' Rivanah was stumped.

'I saw you at the convocation ceremony in Kolkata.'

'Oh!' She could feel a cold sweat forming right behind her ears. 'Thanks,' she managed to say. *What else did he see? Ishita and me following him to his cousin Hiya's place?* she wondered as Argho moved on.

Once she was back at her cubicle, they exchanged a few casual glances, but nothing out of the ordinary. Rivanah was slightly embarrassed by the thought that if Argo was really the Stranger, then he had seen her in all kinds of nudity; both physical and emotional. How do you face a person in that case? Later in the day, she somehow controlled the itch to keep an eye on him, reminding herself that all will be clear in a week's time. *One week*, Rivanah leaned back on her chair and wondered, *and finally the whole mystery will end.* Talking of mysteries, it struck her that she should continue sketching if she knew the craft. The sketches at her place told her she wasn't exactly a novice. But one more issue still remained: why did she forget about the sketches, like she had forgotten about Hiya?

'Come on, let's go,' Rivanah heard one of her team members say. She opened her eyes and sat up straight on her chair and saw most of the employees rushing off somewhere. She quickly caught up with one of them.

'What happened? Fire drill?' Rivanah tried to guess.

'No, yaar,' Rekha, her teammate, said. 'You weren't here last week. It was announced that Samir Bajaj would deliver a lecture on successful business start-ups. He is here.'

'Samir Bajaj?'

'The entrepreneur of the year: Samir Bajaj. Of Bajaj Corps.'

'Oh,' Rivanah said, making a face as she followed Rekha to the boardroom. The whole thing sounded dead boring to her.

The boardroom was packed with employees, making Rivanah feel claustrophobic. The two chairs in the centre were reserved for Samir Bajaj and the CEO of her company, Anil Khanna. There were a few mineral-water bottles kept in the front, a bouquet and couple of small trays with Ferrero Rochers on it. They were her weakness. She went near the chairs and as others were busy chit-chatting and tapping on their mobile phones Rivanah picked up a handful of chocolates and stealthily went and stood in a corner.

The lecture was exactly as Rivanah had predicted: BORING. Sometime in the middle of it, she managed to step out of the boardroom, popped one of the chocolates into her mouth and went back to her cubicle. There was nobody in the entire floor except for few office boys. She had last seen Argho in the boardroom with his colleagues. Rivanah thought of checking her Facebook but what she saw on her desktop monitor made her go numb. A Word doc was open and had bold, red-coloured words in font size 36:

It's farewell, Mini.

Before she knew, Rivanah was already sweating in the air-conditioned floor of her office. Out of fear, she walked briskly to the boardroom again. She didn't dare to turn and check if anyone was watching or following her. The moment she entered the boardroom, she heard people applauding. The session was finally over. She noticed Argho on the opposite side. He did look at her but Rivanah couldn't guess if it was an intentional gaze or a casual one. Mr Bajaj and Mr Khanna walked out of the boardroom together. Everyone else started to file out too. Once the crowd became thin, she went towards the exit only to be stopped by someone.

'You left these,' the man said. He had few Ferrero Rochers in his hand. It was the same greenish-eyed man who had saved her in the elevator and once more in the backstairs. He had an amused expression on his face; he had obviously seen Rivanah stealing the other Ferrero Rochers from the plate.

'I'm sorry. Actually, I can't resist these,' she said apologetically.

'It's okay. Stealing chocolates isn't a crime.' He flashed a smile and Rivanah's mind buzzed with a new-crush alert. She took the chocolates from him.

'Thanks,' she said.

The man turned and started walking away, when she stopped him saying, 'Excuse me! I'm Rivanah Bannerjee.' She extended her hand for a handshake.

'Call me Nivan,' he said and shook her hand with a firmnesss that evoked certain forbidden thoughts in Rivanah's mind. Before she could follow him further to know which department he worked in, she remembered she had something more important waiting. Rivanah called Sadhu Ram, clicked a picture of the Word document on her screen, and sent it to him on WhatsApp as directed. He asked her to be extra alert.

Rivanah was expecting a call from Sadhu Ram but it didn't come. She left office early and took a cab home. She noticed a bike was always moving parallel to her cab. The rider whose head was hidden inside a mercury-coated helmet kept looking sideways. Rivanah's heart was in her mouth. There was no prize for guessing who this rider could be. What if he attacked her? She rolled up the window of the cab and asked the driver to go faster, but it didn't matter how fast he drove, the rider was always parallel to her. Did he come to know about the police guy following him? Rivanah was getting nervous with every passing second. She kept Sadhu Ram's number open on her phone.

Finally, at one of the traffic signals, the rider halted right next to Rivanah's cab and climbed down the bike. Her heart almost stopped. She checked if the cab's door was locked; it was. The rider came right up to the window and removed his helmet. It was Ekansh. For a moment, she didn't know how to react. Next, out of rage, she rolled down the cab's window. But before Rivanah could ask him why the hell he was stalking her like a fool, he said, 'I have found a way to apologize to Tista.'

Somehow he didn't look like his former self.

10

'What the hell are you talking about, Ekansh?' Rivanah said. Before she could get around to asking him why he was following her, the traffic light turned green. Vehicles behind them were honking, with drivers hurling abuses at them for holding up the traffic on a busy street. Ekansh wasn't ready to go back to his bike. Rivanah didn't know what to do, nor did the cab driver. He kept inching the cab ahead while Ekansh kept jogging alongside.

'Ekansh!' Rivanah rebuked, 'Get your damn bike and meet me at the other side of the signal.' To the driver she said, 'Bhaiya, signal ke aage side kar dijiye.'

The cab driver mentally abused Ekansh for cutting his drive short. Once he crossed the signal and parked the car, Rivanah paid the fare and got down. Ekansh by then had parked his bike right behind the cab. She went straight to him.

'What's your problem, Ekansh?'

'Rivanah, I'm sorry,' he said, removing his helmet once again.

'Why are you doing this to me? We are done. Like *done*! Let's not re-establish contact ever again.'

'Can we please sit and talk?'

'No! We can't!' Rivanah was furious. She looked around only to realize her pitch was loud enough to attract attention. Heads were turning in their direction. It made her uncomfortable.

'Okay, let's go,' she said.

She wanted to be done with this once and for all. Rivanah rode pillion as they headed to the nearest CCD outlet.

'Tell me, what is it?' Rivanah snapped, once Ekansh had placed his order.

'Firstly, I'm sorry,' Ekansh said.

'Your sorry irritates me, Ekansh. You always say sorry but you are never really sorry. So please cut the crap and tell me why you were following me. You were saying something about Tista?'

'I couldn't sleep after Tista passed away. I felt restless all the time thinking that Tista knew what happened and I couldn't even say sorry to her.'

'Again sorry? Listen, you either come straight to the point or I'm out of here.'

Ekansh understood that Rivanah was losing patience. 'I won't be able to live in peace if I don't apologize to her.'

Rivanah stared at Ekansh like he had lost it completely. 'Didn't Tista die in front of both of us?'

Ekansh nodded.

'Then what is this "I want to apologize to her" bullshit?'

'Planchette.'

'What?' Her disbelief pushed her to reconfirm with him.

'I will call upon her soul and apologize.'

She knew what a planchette was. Once or twice during college, some friends had talked about it eagerly, but nobody had ever tried it. Rivanah didn't even know if it was real. *Can souls be really recalled?* Rivanah knew she couldn't be a part of this nonsense.

'Ekansh, I can't help you in this, and please don't follow me or try to contact me again. I'm sorry for whatever happened with Tista, I really am, but I too have a life. Let me live it peacefully,' she said and started to walk away.

'Don't you want to apologize to Tista too?' he asked. His high pitch made the other customers look at them with curiosity. She gave him a you-are-incorrigible look and stormed out.

Rivanah knew she was being rude but she didn't care. To cut all ties, one had to be rude at times. She had already tried it the other way and it hadn't worked.

Once Rivanah reached home, she called Danny. He didn't answer but a minute later messaged that he was in a meeting and would call back right after it ended. Loneliness brought the memory of Tista. Her face started flashing in front of Rivanah along with Ekansh's last words to her: *Don't you want to apologize too?* Ekansh's guilt was spreading its roots deep in her as well. She had chosen to ignore it, Ekansh hadn't. But now, after meeting him, she was forced to pay attention to it. And who was responsible for this guilt? Who had told Tista about the unplanned 'escapade' between Ekansh and her?

Rivanah called up Sadhu Ram. 'Sadhu Ramji, any news yet?'

'Just been two hours. As of now, nothing. Argho Chowdhury lives in Andheri East. I'm right outside his building.'

'All right.'

'Don't worry, I shall let you know if I get anything.'

'Okay, thank you.'

Rivanah thought of messaging the Stranger; it didn't matter to her then if it was Argho. He owed her an explanation as to why he had told Tista and made everyone's life miserable. Including the one who was dead.

Why did you tell Tista the truth? Rivanah tapped her phone hard to write the message and sent it to all the numbers she had saved of the Stranger.

Why didn't you tell Danny the truth? came the Stranger's reply. Rivanah frowned, reading the message, and dialled the number from which she had received it, pressing her phone against her ears.

'Hello, Mini,' the Stranger said in a male voice.

'Get this right: I will not tell Danny the truth, okay?'

'Then I will,' the Stranger replied in a poised manner.

'You will not!' Rivanah brought the phone in front of her mouth and almost screamed at it.

'I sure will.' The tone remained unaffected.

A few seconds of silence later, Rivanah added, 'Please. I beg you. I'm done with Ekansh. Telling Danny the truth may not go well. I just don't want to take a chance.'

'If you don't take a chance, you will never know how true your love is.'

'I already know how true our love is, so please spare me.'

'You have no idea, Mini, how much these assumptions of yours excite me to prove you otherwise.'

Rivanah swallowed a lump.

'You are simply impossible,' she said and hung up.

The next second the Stranger messaged back: *Guilty as charged.* A pissed-off Rivanah put her phone away and opened her laptop to distract herself. There was no way she was going to tell Danny about what had happened between Ekansh and her. Definitely not now, when everything was back on track between Danny and her. She was about to log in to her Facebook when another message popped up on her phone.

Please!

It was a WhatsApp from Ekansh. Rivanah didn't care to reply. She put her phone on silent mode and continued logging on to Facebook. She checked her phone again. There was a missed call from Ekansh. *This guy has turned nuts! Does he really think I will help him with . . .*

74

what was the word . . . planchette? She wondered and, after
a thoughtful moment, typed the word on Google. For
the next one hour, Rivanah read whatever Google had
to offer on planchette. And most of them were real life
incidents—or so the articles claimed. There was one
particular article which piqued her interest the most. It
said that a planchette was done by a group of relatives to
connect with the spirit of a person who was murdered.
And they claimed that through planchette they identified
who the murderer was. It sounded like a television script
but it intrigued her. Could it be true? If yes, then all her
problems would end in one go. Was it worth a try? What
will she lose even if it's a bluff? Rivanah picked up her
phone and stared at Ekansh's name for some time before
finally dialling his number. He answered on the second
ring itself.

'Hi. I knew you would call.'

She ignored the comment and came straight to the
point.

'I shall help you communicate with Tista, but I have
a condition.'

'What condition?'

'You too will have to help me communicate with
someone.'

'Who?'

'Hiya Chowdhury.'

11

The plan seemed perfect. Rivanah would go to Ekansh's place right after office. And together they would call upon the spirit of Tista first and then Hiya through planchette, and help each other get rid of their personal burdens. Ekansh wanted to apologize while Rivanah wanted to ask Hiya who her killer was. Ekansh enquired why she wanted to know who killed Hiya when the entire college knew she committed suicide; Rivanah simply put forward her second condition: no questions. But she didn't let Ekansh go without asking him a few questions of her own.

'Was Hiya my friend?' she asked.

'She was your batchmate. The topper.'

'What else do you know about Hiya and me?'

'What do you mean?'

'Just answer me, Ekansh.'

'Nothing more. But why are you asking me? Whatever I know, you too should know, right? In fact, you would know more since she was your batchmate, not mine.'

Rivanah didn't answer. Now, standing by the window of her bedroom, she wondered how she could answer something she didn't remember about herself.

Danny called for her attention.

'Can we go for dinner tomorrow night? Maybe I'll get free early,' he said, sipping on green tea while phone-browsing.

'Sure, we can.' She didn't want to refuse now and raise an alarm. But she knew that she would have to call Danny after work and, on the pretext of an important meeting, go straight to Ekansh's place to finish the chapter of the Stranger's identity once and for all. Then she would come back to be with Danny. Forever. *Forever: the root of all flowery assumptions in a love story*, she thought and knew no one could severe oneself from this concept since it is forever that makes the fight for love worth it. Somewhere, the fact that she was ready to remain committed to Danny forever helped her justify her lie to him. And what was the truth anyway? That Ekansh and she had fucked that night in the flat? It was one of those random slips which . . . Rivanah checked her thoughts . . . well, it wasn't a random slip. Such vulnerability towards someone happens when that someone defines almost the whole of your past. And more often than not, it is a permanent vulnerability. After all, time isn't a strong-enough detergent to wash off certain spots of memories.

The planchette though, Rivanah thought, *was her best bet to clean up her life once and for all.* First, she wouldn't meet

Ekansh ever again after this, and second, she would know who the Stranger is since she was sure he was the one who had killed Hiya. She would then move on with Danny to happier and less-confusing times.

The next day Rivanah went to her office on time. Seeing Argho reminded her that she had received no intimation from Sadhu Ram. She wanted to call him but stopped herself, deciding it was better to give Sadhu Ram his own time. Not like he would hold on to information. Tonight something would anyway come up. Only nine hours remained before they dabbled in planchette.

In the afternoon, she received a message from Ekansh asking if their plan was still on. She wanted to clarify that it was his plan, and that she was only helping him, but sent a dry 'yes' instead. She didn't want to give him any signal to lurch on to and initiate something which may progress into anything even remotely close to a relationship.

After work, Rivanah called Danny and told him she had a meeting and wouldn't be able to join him for dinner. But she promised she would prepare his favourite dish the moment she was home. Danny said he would wait. Rivanah took a cab and rushed to Ekansh's place. He was putting up at an out-of-town friend's place in Santa Cruz.

Ekansh opened the door before Rivanah could press the doorbell.

'I saw you coming into the building,' Ekansh said. She gave him a tight smile noticing his dark circles were more pronounced than ever but chose not to comment. He looked desperate. She didn't know what weighed on him more—Tista's death or his guilt. *Did our break up ever weigh on him?* Rivanah thought and stepped into the rather tiny flat.

'You want to drink some water?' he said.

'Let's go through this quickly, please.'

Ekansh looked at her and nodded.

'I have arranged everything. Come on in,' he said.

After a slight hesitation she followed him inside. It was a small, dimly lit bedroom with no furniture. A rolled-up mattress lay in one corner. In the middle of the room, she noticed, was the Ouija board used for planchette, as Google had told her a day back. It was an ancient portal to connect to the dead. Till that moment, she had been eager, but now, as she saw the Ouija board, she felt scared. Would Tista's and Hiya's spirit actually come to them? Her throat went bone dry.

'I need some water,' she told Ekansh. He was busy placing a candle at each corner of the Ouija board.

'Sure.' He stood up and went out of the bedroom. Rivanah came forward and knelt down to notice a coin at the centre of the board. There was a sound and Rivanah's heart was in her mouth. She turned to see Ekansh bringing her a glass of water.

'I'm sorry.' He realized he had petrified Rivanah.

'It's okay.' It was not. She nervously took the glass of water from him and gulped it down in one go.

'So how do we go about it?'

Ekansh kept the glass away and sat down beside the Ouija board. He took a deep breath and said, 'We both sit opposite each other.'

Rivanah sat down right opposite Ekansh. He brought one of the corner candles and put it at the centre of the board and said, 'We need to put our index fingers on the coin.' He put his finger on it. Rivanah followed. He stretched his hand saying, 'We must hold our hands.'

Rivanah wasn't sure.

'It's important, Rivanah.'

Reluctantly she stretched her hand. Ekansh clasped it.

'We need to close our eyes and call upon whom we want to first.'

'Tista.' Rivanah wanted to say Hiya's name first but the hair on her nape had stood up at the thought of it.

'We need to call Tista to our mind with utmost attention and focus.'

'How will we know she is here?'

'This candle will extinguish on its own,' he said, glancing at the candle in the centre.

On its own . . . the thought made Rivanah's tension rise up, shortening her breaths.

'And with these letters and numbers, we can interact with her,' Ekansh said, gesturing at the Ouija board. Rivanah swallowed a lump. *How can Ekansh be so cool about all this?* she thought. He looked like he dealt with spirits on a regular basis. Perhaps he was more concerned about his apology than anything else. *Typically selfish Ekansh*, Rivanah concluded.

'Let's close our eyes and start chanting her name,' he said and closed his eyes. Rivanah too closed her eyes and together in their minds they started chanting Tista's name. Rivanah started having flashes of all the good times she had spent with Tista, especially that scene with her questioning eyes, as she looked at her before going in for the surgery. She could never forget those eyes. They had an accusation in them, as if her trust had been breached. And rightly so. Had she not let the sexual slip happen with Ekansh that evening in the flat then . . . Rivanah felt Ekansh's grasp tighten. On an impulse, she opened her eyes and found him staring at the candle. Its flame had died. Rivanah could hear her own heart beating. Her body was mildly shivering. Was it real? Was Tista's spirit in the room? Suddenly she felt a haunting energy in the room. It freaked her out.

'Tista, are you there?' Ekansh spoke up. He sounded brittle. Rivanah didn't move. She only kept moving her eye balls from right to left, scared to see an apparition. She suddenly felt Ekansh pushing her finger which was on the coin. And before she could even fight it, the coin was already moved to the right, to the space in the Ouija board marked 'yes'. One glance at Ekansh and she knew he wasn't pushing the coin at will. Or was he? There was something eerie in the air and Rivanah felt she couldn't breathe any more. Her hands and legs felt heavy and muscles stiff.

'I'm sorry, Tista,' he said. Rivanah could sense his lips shiver and voice shudder as he spoke, 'I know I broke your trust. But I'm apologizing now.'

Nothing happened.

'Will you please—?'

One of the windows in the room opened suddenly. Rivanah was about to stand up but Ekansh held on to her tightly. She was profusely sweating by now. *I'm not doing this again*, Rivanah promised herself, as she heard Ekansh speak again. She had never felt her heart beating so hard.

'Will you please forgive me, Tista? I love you and I mean it.' Ekansh was staring at the coin hoping it would move to his left. A moment later, their fingers on the coin felt a push to the 'yes' part of the board. Was it really a spirit or was it Ekansh's own guilt manipulating him to push the coin, Rivanah couldn't tell.

'Thank you so much, Tista, for liberating me from this guilt. I miss you.'

Rivanah was glaring at Ekansh. He understood why.

'Goodbye, Tista,' he said and the next moment he let Rivanah's hand go.

'Are we done?' she whispered.

'Yes. Should we call upon Hiya?'

'No!' Rivanah stood up.

'What happened?'

'I changed my mind. And I'm leaving.'

Ekansh could tell she was scared. Rivanah walked to the drawing room with Ekansh behind her. *It was a foolish idea to even participate in this*, she thought. One more minute, and she would have fainted there.

'What's the matter, Rivanah?'

'Nothing. And, by the way, we are now officially done. Please don't try to contact me.'

'I thought we—'

'Just don't do that, Ekansh. We are done. Period,' she said and was about to storm out when her phone rang. It was Danny. She gestured Ekansh to keep quiet, with a finger on her lips, and took the call.

'Hey, baby.' For Danny, she was having a long day at office. She tried her best to sound tired.

'Hey, where are you?'

'Office. I told you I have a long meeting.'

'Hmm.' He didn't sound convinced.

'What happened?'

'Someone just messaged me saying you are with Ekansh at his place. I was pretty confident you weren't, but I was passing by your office, so thought I'd stop over.'

How could she underestimate this 'someone', Rivanah cursed herself and said, 'Where are you now?'

'I'm right outside your office. Can you come out for a minute?'

Rivanah pressed the mute button quickly and looking at Ekansh said, 'You need to help me out. Fast!'

12

'Give me five minutes. I'll be downstairs,' Rivanah told Danny on phone and disconnected. She wasn't sure if it was Argho who had messaged Danny, but she decided she would take care of it later. First, she had to reach Danny.

'But we can't reach your office in five minutes,' Ekansh said, picking up his friend's bike keys from the key holder near the main door.

'We'll have to,' Rivanah said and rushed out of the flat. Ekansh followed.

They zoomed to her office on Ekansh's friend's bike. The traffic was intense and they had to stop at almost every signal. Rivanah's tension grew by the minute as she constantly kept checking the time on her watch. *What if Danny calls back? With such a cacophony of horns all around, he'll immediately know I'm not inside the office.* Four minutes after they had left, they had only crossed half the distance. She told Ekansh to speed up. He looked at her via the rear-view mirror and changed the gear. He didn't stop at any signal even though most were red. When they were just one traffic signal away from her office, Ekansh was cornered by three traffic policemen.

'Damn! Not now,' Rivanah lamented. As Ekansh stopped his bike and took off his helmet, he turned around and said, 'You take an auto and leave. I'll sort this out.'

Rivanah didn't waste another second. While she was climbing down the bike, Danny called again. She let the phone ring for a bit while she hailed an autorickshaw and then cut the call. She immediately WhatsApped him:

Two minutes, baby. Meeting is getting over.

Okay.

She prayed hard that she would make it on time. *No more Ekansh. No more visiting the past. No more lies to Danny.* Rivanah didn't like one bit of what she was doing. And to negate the dislike, she kept telling herself, *I will make up for it. I really will.*

As the autorickshaw took a turn from the Linking Road signal, she noticed a Xylo near the main gate of her office building. Danny was sitting on the driver's seat perusing his phone. Even if she wanted to, she couldn't afford to get down from the autorickshaw there. She asked the driver to go around the office building and eventually got down near the back gate. She paid the fare and WhatsApped Danny:

Where are you? I'm at the back gate.

Oh, I'm at the front. Wait, I'm coming, Danny replied. Waiting for him, Rivanah wondered what a fool she had been to have involved herself with Ekansh for the planchette. *Like always!* Every time she convinced herself

85

she had improved, she ended up doing some stupid act or the other. And her instinct told her it would continue till she was done with Hiya. Or maybe till Hiya was done with her. She would have herself died of fear in Ekansh's flat had she been there for a minute longer. She wanted to know who had killed Hiya Chowdhury and who the Stranger was, but not this way. This way, she would only die and join Hiya wherever she was. Rivanah saw a Xylo taking a turn on the back lane. She waved and walked towards it.

'I had a talk with Sadhu Ram,' Danny said the moment Rivanah got into the car and wore her seat belt. She looked at him expectantly.

'He said Argho is presently at his flat in Andheri. I also passed him the number from which I received the message. Sadhu Ram got it checked. It came from the tower closest to Argho's place.'

'Goddamn it! Can't we just get him?'

'I asked him the same thing. But we need more definite clues to round Argho up since the number wasn't registered in his name.'

'Oh!' She took Danny's phone and checked the message:

Rivanah is alone with Ekansh at his friend's flat in Santa Cruz.

She swallowed a lump because every word of it was true. She checked the number next. A chill ran through her spine. It was Ekansh's Mumbai number which, she was sure, the Stranger had duplicated and used to message Danny.

'Do you recognize the number?' Danny asked.

Rivanah shook her head hesitatingly.

'I ran it via Truecaller. It did throw up a name—Ekansh,' he said.

Rivanah frowned as if it was news to her.

'Anyway, where do you want to go for dinner?' Danny asked, shifting the gear.

'Home.'

'Huh?'

'Remember, I'm supposed to prepare dinner for us tonight,' she said smiling.

'Oh yes. Sounds super.'

Rivanah leaned back on her seat, switched on the FM to a channel which was playing a soft romantic number and tried to relax, hoping Danny would not probe further, when she heard him speak.

'Don't take it otherwise, Rivanah, but is there something that I should know but you aren't telling me?'

Rivanah glanced at him not knowing how or where to hide her emotions. *Yes, there are things I haven't told you yet. But, trust me, they aren't important. Not any more. Those things involve me—and only me. I know what involves one involves the other too in a relationship, but, trust me, I won't let it affect what we share with each other.* She locked her jaws tight in order to gulp her emotions before they made their presence obvious.

'Has that scoundrel been disturbing you a lot?' he asked.

Rivanah spoke after a pause, 'Not really.'

'What do you mean?'

'I think he knows I have been to the police so I haven't heard anything from him again. Nothing after the kerosene episode.'

'Hmm.'

Danny surprised Rivanah by clasping her hand gently. He looked at her as he drove on a rather empty lane.

'I don't want a veil between you and me, Rivanah. If we love each other, we shouldn't have filters. You get my point?'

Do I get his point? Or do I already know what he means but can't believe in it enough to implement it? But Rivanah found herself nodding in agreement. The only filter that love is capable of building in us is secrecy. When we are in love, we don't want our own selves to be an enemy of our relationship. And the more we stick to this want, the more vehemently the filter of secrecy is built. Though it is to protect something we long to have—the relationship—it is also potent enough to destroy it.

Once they reached their flat, Rivanah went to the kitchen to prepare lemon rice and pepper chicken, which they had with red wine. Every time Danny appreciated the preparation, Rivanah's guilt got a massage. Done with dinner, she went closer to him and, making herself comfortable in his lap, wine glass in hand, asked, 'Danny, you know I love you, right?'

'Yeah? I never knew that! Mind explaining?' he said, with an amused smile.

Rivanah looked into his eyes and held his chin in her hand, tilting his face a bit, and then planted a hard kiss on his lips. The moment their tongues met, she pushed herself inside his mouth and within seconds squeezed the blood out of his lips.

'You want more proof, mister?' This time a wicked amusement reflected in her face.

'I don't mind,' Danny said, maintaining eye contact. Rivanah slowly emptied the entire glass of red wine over his forehead and then started tracing it as the wine cascaded down his face. She licked his forehead, his cheeks, his ears, his chin and finally she came back to his lips from where she sucked the blood out from the tiny wound she had made seconds back. They were about to smooch again when Rivanah's phone rang. She pursed Danny's lips as she picked up her phone. He broke the kiss and asked, 'Who is it?'

Rivanah cut the call and said, 'Nobody.' She proceeded to kiss him when the phone rang again and Ekansh's name appeared on the screen. Danny caught Rivanah glancing at the phone in a spiteful way.

'Why don't you just take it?'

Rivanah understood even Danny was affected by it as much as she was. She picked up on the last ring.

'I'm sorry to disturb you, Rivanah . . .'

When will he stop using that goddamn sorry word! Rivanah wondered.

'I came out with you in a hurry,' Ekansh said over phone. 'I forgot my driver's licence. And now they have locked me up at the Goregaon police station.'

'What?' Rivanah couldn't hide her shock.

'Could you please come and bail me out?' Ekansh said. 'I called all my friends here in Mumbai. Nobody is available right now. The ones in Navi Mumbai will take forever to reach.'

'Uh-huh.' Rivanah kept shooting furtive glances at Danny trying to maintain a calm demeanour.

'Okay,' she said.

'Thanks a lot.'

'Okay. See you in some time. Bye.' She hung up and gave an exasperated look at Danny.

'Office call and you have to go,' he said.

Rivanah nodded.

'Then why are you looking so guilty about it? Work first. Should I drop you? It's already eleven.'

'I will take an auto or a cab. Don't worry. I'll be back soon. And . . .' she took his face in her hands and, kissing his nose, said, 'I will make up for this real soon.'

'You better! And be safe. Call if need be,' Danny said. *Only a woman knows how much a man's concern can turn her on*, she thought.

'I will,' she said, kissing the tip of his nose with a smile.

Soon Rivanah was in a cab heading towards the Goregaon police station. The traffic had eased out in the last hour. As her cab took a left turn from Mega Mall, a biker joined them from behind. The biker had his head covered with a helmet just like Ekansh had a day before.

What the fuck! Rivanah thought. *When will this guy understand we are done with each other?* She asked the driver to stop the cab. The driver slowed down first and then halted the cab on the left. Rivanah got down immediately and turned to see the biker had stopped right behind the cab.

'What's wrong with you, Ekansh?' In the calmness of the night, it sounded like a shout even though it wasn't quite.

The biker rode the bike to reach her.

'What? Will you explain this?' she said, first shrugging and then putting both her hands on her hips.

'You are going to have it from me if you tell me you lied about the lock-up thing.' The biker didn't move except for stretching his right hand towards her. His fist was closed. She noticed the biker was wearing gloves. A familiar smell reached her—Just Different, Hugo Boss. Rivanah's heartbeats slowed down. His fist opened and . . . *Is he going to slash my throat?* Rivanah thought and felt her knees lose strength by the second. The hand caressed her cheeks. She saw something drop to the ground. She looked down. It was a white piece of cloth. Before she could lift her head, she heard the biker speed away. There was no way to note down the number on the plate. It was only seconds after the biker left that Rivanah regained her composure and picked up the white cloth. In black embroidery it read:

People use love to justify their dishonesty. You ONLY have two more days to confess, Mini.

13

'Madam, chalna hai ki nahi?' the cab driver asked, realizing Rivanah was standing like a fool even after the rider had long gone.

Rivanah nodded and got into the cab again. *Was it Argho? Is he really going to tell Danny the truth if I don't confess in two days?* Rivanah kept wondering as the cab drove to the Goregaon police station. Standing outside the station entrance, for a moment Rivanah didn't know why she was there. Her phone buzzed with Danny's call. She picked it up on an impulse.

'Did you reach office?' Danny asked.

'No,' Rivanah blurted.

'What? It's been half an hour. Didn't you get a cab or what?'

It was then that she remembered the lie she had cooked up and made up an excuse for her slip up, 'I meant I'm about to enter the office building.'

'Oh, okay. Call me once you leave. I'm not sleeping until you are back.'

'Sure.'

Rivanah cut the call, paid the cab driver and then got out of the cab. She went straight inside the police station.

There were two vest-clad constables sitting and laughing outside a lock-up. The old man inside the lock-up, a convict by the looks of it, too was laughing with the constables. There was no sign of Ekansh. Rivanah went to the inspector sitting with his legs on the table and flipping through a foreign issue of *Maxim*. Rivanah coughed to get the inspector's attention. He looked up at her, startled. He kept the magazine aside and withdrew his legs from the table, shooting an inquiring look at Rivanah.

'I'm here to meet Ekansh Tripathi,' Rivanah said. The inspector's reply was blocked out by the beep of a WhatsApp message on her phone. It was from Ekansh:

Thank you.

'Please excuse me,' Rivanah told the inspector and called up Ekansh.

'Hey, nice to get your call,' Ekansh said picking up the phone.

'Where the hell are you?'

'I'm on my way home. Why?'

'Who bailed you out?' Rivanah asked. By then she had already started walking away from the inspector and towards the entrance. The inspector kept staring at Rivanah cluelessly.

'You sent a lawyer and bailed me out ten minutes ago.'

'What?'

'Why are you sounding so surprised?'

'Did you tell anyone about the incident except me?'

'No. Why would I?'

Only one person could have known where Ekansh was.

'Is something up?' Ekansh asked.

The inspector saw Rivanah step out of the police station. He was too lazy to ask her why she was there in the first place. He picked up the magazine again.

'No, nothing,' Rivanah said and continued, 'Ekansh, I want you to listen carefully to what I'm about to say next.'

'I'm listening.'

'I want you to delete my number after I disconnect this call. Whatever we shared—good, bad, ugly—it is all in the past and we should put it behind us and move on. Do you get what I'm trying to tell you?'

'Hmm. You don't want us to be in touch any more.'

'Precisely.'

'But I need you, Rivanah.'

Rivanah rolled her eyes and continued, 'Please don't say things like that. When you had me, you never needed me. Now when you can't have me, you shouldn't need me.'

'But—'

'Ekansh, this is for our own good. I expect you to understand this and ask no further questions. Stay good.'

'So this is it? We become strangers?'

The last word sent a shiver down Rivanah's spine. What if the Stranger was watching her?

'Yes, this is it. We don't become strangers. We simply stop believing the fact that we are not an option for each other any more.'

There was silence at the other end.

'Goodbye, Ekansh. Take care,' Rivanah said, expecting a reply but he said nothing. She disconnected the line. A few seconds later, she deleted Ekansh's number as well as his chat messages from her phone. She looked around for a cab but couldn't find any. She opened her phone and tapped on the Ola app. There was a cab available within 5 minutes. While booking the cab, she heard something and looked up. At a distance, there was a bike with its headlights on. The rider was intentionally accelerating the bike to draw attention. In the darkness, she couldn't tell who it was and yet she knew it could only be one person. Her phone rang with an unknown number. She swallowed a lump and put the phone against her ears.

'Hello, Mini,' said a man's voice.

'What do you want?' Rivanah's voice was shivering.

'I want you to know your own worth, Mini.'

'That's what you have been telling me for a long time now. I want a different answer. And a correct one.'

There was silence. Rivanah was looking straight at the biker and knew the person would have his eyes on her.

'So, you won't answer?' she asked.

'So, you won't confess?' the Stranger shot back.

Rivanah became quiet for few seconds and then said, 'I will confess, but I want something in return. You can't always push me to do anything you want.' Though Rivanah was putting forth a condition, she couldn't sound confident about it.

'What is it?'

'I want to see you. As in, I want to see your face.'

There was silence at the other end.

'The moment you reveal your identity to me, I shall confess to Danny,' Rivanah said, knowing it was akin to Hobson's choice for the Stranger, so even though he was being given the freedom to make a free choice, only one option was actually being offered. There was no way the person on the bike was going to reveal his identity to her. Finally she had trapped the Stranger in some sort of dilemma. Her face broke into a sly smile.

'I shall meet you, Mini.'

The smile disappeared from Rivanah's face.

'You mean you are going to reveal your identity?'

'I shall reveal my identity to you.'

Rivanah swallowed hard and said, 'Now?'

'Soon. You will know when I do.'

'But no tricks. No masks. No nothing.'

'Promise. No tricks. No masks. No nothing,' the Stranger said.

'I'll wait,' Rivanah said and noticed her Ola cab had come up. The biker switched the headlight off and allowed the darkness to absorb him.

Rivanah got into the cab and was on her way to her flat.

'Bhaiya, AC on kar dijiye please,' she told the driver wiping the sweat off her brow.

'Madam, AC on hai,' the driver said.

And yet she was sweating profusely. She took out the wet, fragranced tissue from her purse and rubbed her face and nape with it. She kept looking behind to see if the Stranger was following her, but could spot no one. Something struck her. She took her phone and dialled Sadhu Ram's number. He picked up the phone and sounded groggy.

'Yes, madam.'

'What is Argho doing now?'

'He came back to his flat two hours back. I'm sitting right outside his apartment gate.'

'Oh okay, thank you,' Rivanah said and cut the line. *Argho can't be the Stranger then,* she thought. What she and Sadhu Ram didn't know was that Argho's bike was missing from the apartment's garage that moment.

14

There was an unusual buzz in Rivanah's office. Everyone, especially her own team members, looked happy and energetic. Rivanah soon found out that one of their important clients was happy with the software that her team had developed and had hence thrown a party for all of them after office hours. The news, however, didn't excite Rivanah much. She would have skipped the party if she had a choice. The moment she sat on the chair in her cubicle, her eyes fell on a pamphlet placed at her desk. It read: *Self-defence classes for women.* She looked around and saw the same pamphlet on every female employee's desk. Rivanah saved the phone number given on the pamphlet and folded it neatly before keeping it in her purse. The place was near her residence. She made a mental note of giving it a shot in a day or two. With the Stranger making his fatal intent clear more than a couple of times, self-defence may come in handy, she thought.

All through the morning, Rivanah kept checking her phone from time to time, constantly debating with herself whether the Stranger would actually reveal his identity to her. And if so, where would they meet? But no message came from the Stranger. It wasn't only about his revelation this time. There was a consequence to the revelation as well. If the Stranger actually revealed his identity, she would have to confess the truth to Danny. The fear of the consequence kept convincing her that the Stranger, as always, wouldn't reveal himself after all. It was one of those ploys of his to put her on the back foot. Rivanah was too mentally preoccupied to pry on Argho during office hours until she received a phone call from Sadhu Ram.

'Why did you call me last night?' Sadhu Ram asked.

'What?' The question had come out too abruptly for Rivanah to make any sense of it.

'What made you call me?'

'I wanted to check if Argho was at home.'

'Why suddenly?'

'Someone had followed me on a bike.'

'Why didn't you tell me this last night?' asked Sadhu Ram.

'I would have but you told me Argho was at his flat, so I thought . . . why, what happened?'

'I'm keeping a track of the kilometres his bike has been driven so that I know if he has driven without me knowing. Last night when I checked, it read 1203 kilometres, and this morning when he drove to office it read 1250 kilometres. And he drove straight from his house to the office which is only twenty kilometres.'

Rivanah was quiet. She knew what Sadhu Ram was hinting at.

'It means he had taken the bike somewhere last night without my knowledge,' Sadhu Ram said.

The obvious interpretation was: Argho *was* the Stranger. For the first time in the morning, she pushed her chair back and stood up to have a look at Argho. He was in his cubicle working with his back to her.

'Hello? Are you there, madam?' Sadhu Ram spoke over the phone.

'Yes, yes, I'm here.' Rivanah sat down on her chair and continued, 'What do we do now?'

'Did you notice anything last night that would prove it was Argho following you on bike?'

Rivanah thought for a moment. She hadn't seen the biker's face or even noticed the model of the bike. In fact, she didn't know Argho had a bike.

'I don't remember much except that the biker's helmet was black.'

'Hmm. That's not much of a help. Please update me immediately if anything happens. Even if you are remotely suspicious of anything, just let me know.'

'I sure will.'

The phone call ended. Rivanah once again glanced at Argho, who was still working, and thought: *If this guy is the Stranger, then he needs to be given the best actor award.*

Before moving out with her team around 8 p.m. to the Little Door eatery in Andheri West, where the client party was supposed to take place, Rivanah called Danny up who told her he too would be late. Rivanah, on one hand, was in no mood to party, but on the other hand, didn't want to go back to an empty home so early. Reluctantly she asked Danny to pick her up on his way home post the party. A part of the pub was cordoned off for the office team. When Rivanah reached there with her teammates it was rather quiet, but within an hour the place started warming up with people, alcohol and music. After Rivanah had her third Budweiser, she excused herself to go to the loo.

Just as she was about to pull up her panties after relieving herself, her phone beeped with a message.

I'm at the party. See you soon.

It was from one of the numbers belonging to the Stranger. Rivanah couldn't get up from the seat. *Is he really out there in the party? Is he someone I know?* Just then she heard a knock on the door.

'Are you done?' a female voice asked.

Rivanah quickly pulled up her panties, flushed and moved out. She washed her hands, wiped it dry and then, taking a deep breath, stepped outside. The music seemed even louder now. Her eyes were zeroing-in on each and every person in the restaurant. Some were drinking by the bar, some were sitting on couches in the corners and some dancing on the floor. The disco lights made it impossible for her to recognize anyone besides her colleagues whose faces she was familiar with. Finally she located Argho. He was by the bar outside in the open where people were allowed to smoke. Rivanah immediately called Sadhu Ram.

'Hello, I just received a message on my phone saying the Stranger is here.' She was careful nobody overheard her.

'Don't worry, I'm already keeping an eye on anyone who so much as approaches you. Just act as if all's well.'

'Thanks,' Rivanah said sounding relieved. She turned around to locate Sadhu Ram but couldn't see him. She turned to see Argho standing right behind her. She would have spilt his drink had he not pulled his hand back on time.

'Oops, sorry,' she said.

'Not a problem. Enjoying the party?'

'Yes.'

'Good. See you around,' said Argho and went inside. *Too casual,* Rivanah thought feeling an urge to keep an eye on him but knew Sadhu Ram was on it anyway. She went up to her teammates and picked up her beer pint which she had left mid-way before excusing herself to the restroom.

'Shots time, everyone!' one of her teammates screamed coming in with a tray full of tequila-shot pegs, lime and salt. Everyone picked up their pegs except for Rivanah.

'Don't tell me you aren't going to have it?' asked Rekha, the teammate she was closest to.

'Not tonight.'

'Not tonight? Then when? Come on!'

'Please . . .'

'If you aren't drinking, I won't either.'

'Don't be a spoilsport, Rivanah,' said another teammate.

'What's happening?' It was their US client, Mark Gems. Everyone stood up seeing him.

'Rivanah says she won't drink,' Rekha complained.

'What?' Mark sounded almost offended.

'No I mean, I—' Rivanah mumbled.

'What if there's a prize? 500 dollars to the one who gulps down the maximum shots!' Mark announced. There was a collective joyous hoot.

Rivanah was in a fix. She couldn't say no to her client while she knew she wouldn't be able to resist the temptation of the tequila shots if she tasted one. *I won't go for more than two*, she promised herself.

'All right,' she said resigning to the situation.

'That's the spirit girl!' Mark said as her teammates lined up in front of the table they had kept the shots on.

'On the count of three . . .' Mark said and continued, '1—2—3!'

There were seven of them, including Rivanah, and each one of them picked up their peg, did a bottoms-up and sucked on the lime dipped in salt. Mark gestured to one of the waiters who readied another set of shots for them. After each round, the pepping continued and the pressure got to Rivanah. After a total of seven rounds, only three people were left. One of them was Rivanah. The taste of tequila diluted her resolve. By the ninth round, only Rivanah and another guy, Sudhir, were left. On the tenth, Rivanah backed out. Sudhir was declared the winner of 500 dollars by Mark.

'Now just make sure Sudhir doesn't take the 500 dollars home. Your drinks are on him,' Mark said, winking at the group. Everyone laughed out.

'Let's burn the floor now. Come on!' Mark said and made the entire group hit the dance floor. Rivanah's head was already reeling. She thought she was in control but in reality she was high from the numerous tequila shots she had consumed. Rivanah wanted to simply sit by a chair outside but she was pulled to the dance floor by Mark.

The in-house DJ changed the song from a slow one to a fast Punjabi number. Rivanah started grooving to the beats of the music with her teammates. The tequila shots had invaded her conscience. The fact that the Stranger could be watching her flew out of her mind. After a long time she was this drunk. Every problem seemed trivial. Every guilt seemed avoidable. She felt as free as a bird. It was almost as if the alcohol had turned her into a child once again and everything in life was only a wish away. Just then her eyes fell on the guy who had saved her twice: once in the elevator, then at the backstairs. He had also noticed her stealing chocolates from the boardroom. Rivanah was having trouble recollecting his name. But she was very clear about one thing: she had a huge crush on him. He was busy chit-chatting with a male colleague by the in-house bar with a drink in his hand. Rivanah stopped dancing.

'What are you looking at?' Rekha screamed in her ears to negate the sound of the music.

'Who is that guy?' Rivanah asked her. Rekha followed her gaze and replied, 'That's Nivan. VP, sales.' Rivanah held her gaze for some time, the way a naughty thought makes you do, and then moved out of the dance floor. Tipsily, she headed straight towards Nivan.

'Excuse me,' she said. Nivan, along with the male colleague, turned to look at her.

'I wanted to thank you,' Rivanah said in a tipsy voice.

Nivan exchanged a clueless look with the male he was talking to.

'What for?' Nivan asked.

'You saved me some time back.'

'OH. KAY,' Nivan said, by now convinced she was extremely drunk.

'I'll get a refill,' the male sitting beside Nivan said and excused himself.

'So I really wanted to pay back tonight,' muttered Rivanah as she tried to stand upright.

'Really?' an amused Nivan asked.

'Yes. By dancing with you. May I?' Saying so, she pulled Nivan to the dance floor. Once there looking at him in the eye, she whispered, 'Thank you.'

Some of the office people had stopped dancing. It was quite a sight after all—Rivanah pulling the VP, sales, to the floor for a dance. But more than being concerned, it was entertainment for them. As if by a divine plan the music turned into a raunchy English number. Rivanah turned around, gyrating her pelvis rather sexually against Nivan. Before Nivan could think of what to do, Rivanah placed his hands on her waist. Though she was inebriated yet his touch made her labia twitch. Her hips were almost rubbing on to his pelvis as she wildly grooved to the English number. Nivan leaned forward and whispered in her ears, 'I'm overwhelmed with your payback. And I think I don't deserve more than this,' he said with a half-smile.

'No more?' Rivanah asked.

'No more,' Nivan said. Looking over at her teammate, Rekha, he said, 'Take care of her.'

'Sure, sir,' Rekha replied, going red in the face.

Nivan excused himself to rejoin the male colleague he had left at the bar.

Rekha took Rivanah outside in the open while she kept blabbering 'I want to pay back Nivan'. Rekha made her sit by a chair and went to get her a glass of water. Rivanah was finding it difficult to focus. If she was drunk before hitting the dance floor, she now felt sloshed. She placed her head on the table in front of her and shut her eyes. She felt like she was levitating in the air. She could hear the DJ had changed the song inside. She was about to stand up to dance on her own when she heard a voice.

'Hello, Mini.'

15

Rivanah kept staring at the blurry image of the person in front of her. She tried hard to make out the face, but everything seemed hazy. The voice was of a male, she was sure of that. Even the face seemed familiar but . . .

'I've been waiting to meet you, Mister Stranger . . .' she slurred.

'I'm here, Mini. Right in front of you. Revealing myself as promised,' the Stranger said.

'But . . . but . . .' She stretched her hand to touch him. She wanted to convince herself it was all real. Her fingertips traced his forehead to his nose to his lips to his chin.

'Who are you?' she asked.

'Who are you, Mini?' he asked back.

'I'm Rivanah Bannerjee.'

'That's only a name, Mini. And names don't define people.'

Rivanah kept looking at the blurry image of the Stranger, wishing she had not drunk so much, wishing she could hug the Stranger and explain that making out with Ekansh was a slip on her part, that she isn't a bad girl, after all, even if she isn't ready to confess anything to Danny yet.

'Do you love me?' she asked. She had no idea why she had asked him that question.

'Love? Does any one of us even know what love is? We all try to understand it. And the point where we think we have understood it is also the point where we let go of the chance to understand it completely.'

'I love Danny,' she said.

'I'm sure you do.'

'I don't want to confess.'

'You'll have to.'

'Why?'

'I told you something in the very beginning, Mini. Do you remember it?'

'What?'

'Know. Your. Worth.'

'Will I ever know my worth?'

'I wouldn't have wasted my time otherwise.'

Rivanah wanted to reach out for his hand but she frowned, hearing someone shout out her name.

'Rivanah!' It was Smita, another colleague of hers. Rivanah turned around.

'You burnt the dance floor, yaar,' Smita said. Rivanah turned back to look at the Stranger.

'Done partying?' She felt someone tap her shoulder. She turned around and saw it was Danny. There was no sight of the Stranger.

'Huh?' Rivanah wasn't ready for Danny. *What is he doing here?*

'Hi, I'm Danny. Rivanah's boyfriend.'

'I'm Smita. Her colleague.'

'Good to meet you, Smita. Is the party over? May I take Rivanah home?'

'Yeah sure. We are wrapping up right now.'

'But I want to stay and talk to him,' a sloshed Rivanah blabbered. Danny and Smita exchanged a clueless glance.

'Talk to whom?' Danny asked.

'Nobody,' Rivanah said. Danny understood how much under the influence of alcohol she was. He helped her into the car and drove straight home.

Next morning, she woke up remembering nothing. The memory of the Stranger coming and talking to her by the bar in the open seemed so distant that she wasn't sure if it was a memory or a wishful thought. When she checked her phone, it had seven missed calls from Sadhu Ram. She looked around for Danny. Before she could locate him, his phone buzzed. It was Sadhu Ram.

'Hello, where are you guys? I have been calling all day.'

'We were sleeping. What happened?'

'I regained consciousness only an hour back. Are you safe?' Sadhu Ram sounded genuinely concerned.

'Yeah, I'm all right. But what do you mean you regained consciousness?'

'I was knocked out last night.'

'Knocked out?'

'I had gone to the washroom while the party was on, after which I don't remember anything. The Little Door guys took me home.'

Shit!

'When I woke up, I was sure something must have happened to you.'

Rivanah was lost in a trance.

'Hello? You there?'

'Yes, I'm here. Where was Argho at the time?'

'He had already moved out of the party. I have already checked. He stayed with a friend in Bandra after he left the party. He has a strong alibi.'

'Does that mean he isn't the—?'

'That's what it seems like as of now. I think it is someone who is very close to you . . .'

Just then Danny came out of the bathroom in his boxers.

'Nothing like a cold shower,' he said and noticed Rivanah holding his phone to her ear.

'Whose call is it?' he asked.

Someone close to you, she thought, and vaguely remembered how Danny had suddenly appeared in front of her at the party.

'Sadhu Ram,' she blurted.

Danny took the phone from her and talked to Sadhu Ram. He recounted the same story to him. Danny hurled his phone on the bed after disconnecting the call and looked at her.

'Did anything happen last night at the Little Door?'

I was talking to the Stranger and then I saw you in his place, Rivanah wondered and said aloud, 'No. I don't remember anything strange.'

'Can you tell me what time I reached the party?' Danny asked in an interrogative tone.

Rivanah said she wouldn't know.

'I thought so. Even if something had happened, you wouldn't be able to tell.'

Rivanah kept staring at Danny as he wore his tee.

'When did you come last night?' she asked. Danny paused for a trice and said, 'I don't remember the exact time. Should be around 12.30. Why?'

'Just like that.'

'I haven't seen you so sloshed before.'

Rivanah hung her face in utter disappointment. She knew she shouldn't have drunk so much. *Damn the client, damn those tequila shots and damn her teammates. And, above all, damn her own self.* She remembered nothing concrete. Not even whether the Stranger had approached her or not. If he had not, then all was fine. But if he had, then she knew what was coming next. She had to respect her part of the deal. She hadn't received any message from the Stranger yet. Rivanah got ready and left for work, hoping against hope that there was more time.

'You were amazing last night,' Smita said. Rivanah immediately threw a what-are-you-talking-about glance at her. Smita took out her phone and showed her a video of Rivanah gyrating her hips against Nivan. She might have enjoyed it the previous night but in the morning it looked plain vulgar to her.

'No, I didn't do that!' she said, feeling flabbergasted to say the least. She took the phone in her hand and watched the entire clip. By the time the video ended, her expression had changed to one of utter embarrassment. *What would Nivan think of me? A cheap despo!* Rivanah immediately deleted the clip.

'Arrey, why did you delete it?' said Smita, snatching the phone back.

'Isn't it obvious?' Rivanah shot back. 'Did I do anything else?'

'Well, after you went and pulled Nivan to the dance floor and danced like crazy with him, I don't think there was much left to do. And it's good you didn't. Your boyfriend was there shortly after.'

'You met Danny?'

'Yes. You are lucky to have such a caring boyfriend.'

'Thanks.' *I indeed am,* Rivanah thought. But first things first.

'Did you say his name was Nivan?' When he had told her his name for the first time, she hadn't registered it, but she was too tongue-tied to ask him again.

'Uh?'

'The guy I danced with last night.'

'Yes. Nivan; VP, sales.'

Oh god! This gets worse. I had a sexy dance with my VP with no memory of it.

'I need to apologize to him.'

'Well, even I think you should, though he didn't look too offended. Still, you never know.'

Rivanah knew where the Sales head's cabin was. She just didn't know who occupied the cabin until today. She excused herself and went straight to the cabin. With every step forward, she felt her heart beating faster. The man inside the cabin wasn't just her senior at work. He was someone on whom she had had a secret schoolgirlish crush.

'Hi sir, I'm sorry for last night. I wasn't in my senses and . . .' Rivanah kept mumbling the apology to herself softly while preparing herself to knock on the door. The moment she knocked, she heard a voice very close to her ears.

'You dance really well.'

Rivanah turned around and saw Nivan standing very closely behind her. Nivan took a step back and she wondered why. She wasn't complaining about the closeness. The thought made her feel guilty but the pleasure in the guilt made her go red in the face.

'Thank you,' she mumbled.

'You're welcome. Please excuse me,' Nivan said. Rivanah moved so he could enter his cabin but the moment he tried to step inside, she stopped him by his arm. He looked back at her. She let go of his hand immediately.

'I'm sorry for this. And for last night,' she said.

'Last night?'

Does he really not remember or is he intentionally pushing it?
'I'm sorry to have pulled you to the dance floor and . . .'
'That's fine. You were drunk. I got that.'
Rivanah smiled at him saying, 'Thanks.'

Nivan went inside his cabin while Rivanah traipsed towards her cubicle like a little girl who had spoken to her crush for the first time. She hoped her apology was enough to take care of the embarrassment she had caused herself and probably him too. She casually checked her phone which displayed a couple of WhatsApp messages from Danny and a message from one of the Stranger's number. She checked the time. It had come a minute back. She stopped dead in her tracks.

I kept my promise, Mini. I was right there in front of you last night. We had a little chit-chat too. Now it's your turn.

Rivanah missed a heartbeat. He must be lying. He couldn't have possibly revealed himself to her when she wasn't in her senses. Or was it all planned? Or was it all a . . .

You are bluffing. She messaged back.

LOL was the response.

Rivanah stared at the message for some time and then typed back:

What was the colour of my dress last night? She waited impatiently for a response.

He replied: *Pink.*

But she was wearing a purple dress . . . Rivanah paused. Her undergarments were pink. Rivanah swallowed hard.

How do you know that? she messaged.

Why do you always forget that I have my ways, Mini?
Did the Stranger really come in front of her?
'Shit!' she blurted out.
'Any problem?' It was Argho. Rivanah was quick to realize she was blocking his way. She shook her head and moved aside to let him pass. And she kept looking at him. When will she know for sure if Argho was the Stranger or not?

Rivanah went back to her cubicle and was about to call Danny and ask him not to believe in any message or call unless it was actually from her. Chances were the Stranger may manipulate Danny the way he did by messaging about her presence in Ekansh's flat the other night. Just then, her desk phone rang. It was from the security guard, informing her that there was a parcel in her name.

'I'm coming,' Rivanah said, put the receiver down and went to the security post.

A large parcel was waiting for her. She took it after signing in the register and then tore it open. It was a white, one-piece dress in floral print. A sudden smile appeared on her face, the kind that happens when you aren't prepared for something but really like it when it happens. Her phone vibrated with a message:

I'm sure you'll look beautiful in this dress.

Rivanah couldn't believe the Stranger had gifted her that dress. She had known the Stranger for a good while but he still didn't stop surprising her. Admiring the dress, she started walking towards her cubicle when she messaged back: *Thank you. But why this gift?*

You should look beautiful when you confess an ugly truth to Danny.

Rivanah paused reading the Stranger's message. Another message popped up precisely then:

Don't disappoint me, Mini.

There was nothing she could think of except: *Why this dress in particular? Why the dramatics?*

The dress is bugged, Mini. I want to hear you confess. The message popped in her phone as if the Stranger had read her mind.

Coming in front of me when I was sloshed wasn't part of the deal. You have cheated me. She messaged back sitting on her chair in her cubicle feeling a restlessness brewing in her.

The deal was that I would come in front of you. Then you would confess. I didn't ask you to drink. My part of the deal is done, Mini. It is time for you to comply.

Rivanah read and re-read the message. No, she can't simply comply, she kept telling herself. A message popped up after some time.

9 p.m. tonight, Bungalow 9, Bandra. I've booked a table for Danny and you.

After Rivanah read the message for the third time, she smiled. It wasn't the end of road for her after all, she thought. She had a plan to catch the Stranger.

She called Danny and told him that she had booked a table for them at Bungalow 9. Danny promised her he would be there directly from work. Next, Rivanah called Sadhu Ram and noted down his email, immediately after which she created a new email address for herself. She couldn't trust anything or any medium any more. She wrote Sadhu Ram an email where she mentioned all the details—from her dress being bugged to the venue and time Danny and she were supposed to meet. She also wanted to clear her doubts regarding a bugged dress. How far should a person be if he wanted to hear a conversation?

Sadhu Ram confirmed that chances were the person would either be inside or just around the restaurant. Rivanah asked him to stay away from the scene in case the Stranger already knew who he was. After sending the last mail to him she sat back in her chair waiting for the clock to strike 9. She stared at the floral dress she had placed on her table.

'That's a lovely one!' Rekha said, seeing the dress. 'Where did you order it from?'

'It's a gift,' Rivanah said with a tight smile. A few seconds later she picked up the dress and tried to feel it. She felt the microphone placed inside the cloth around the shoulder. The Stranger had taken the trouble to not only buy the dress but stitch the microphone inside. Rivanah sighed. Tonight she would finally know who the Stranger was.

16

Rivanah reached Bungalow 9 before Danny. She had changed into the floral dress in her office itself. She was escorted by one of the restaurant managers to the table reserved. She looked around to see if she could locate any familiar face but found none. Rivanah settled down and ordered a beer to calm her nerves. She kept checking her phone with every sip. Around 9.15 p.m., Danny was escorted inside by the same manager. As he came to the table, Rivanah stood up. They hugged, pecked each other on the cheek and took their seats.

'You look lovely,' Danny complimented.

'Thank you.'

'Why don't I remember you buying this dress?'

'That's because I bought it today itself. I wanted to literally look like your better half.'

'You look way better, my better half,' Danny said and leaned forward to kiss her cheek again.

A waiter came and placed the beverage menu on the table along with the food menu. Danny took the former while Rivanah picked up the latter.

'I want some red wine,' Danny said and looked at Rivanah inquiringly.

'I'm done drinking for the night,' she said sipping the last bit of beer from her pint. She couldn't afford to get drunk tonight.

'You suddenly sound so health conscious,' Danny said and added, 'Remember how you used to go to the gym once?'

'Yes,' Rivanah said. The time when the two had connected for the first time seemed long time ago.

'I never went there to get a good figure,' she said with a naughty amusement on her face.

'Is it? Then what for?' Danny responded with the same naughtiness in her tone.

'I wanted to set my life right,' she said and blew him a kiss.

Rivanah helped Danny choose his red wine while she zeroed-in on a sushi platter.

Danny picked up his glass of red wine and gestured at her. Rivanah knew how Danny would do a 'cheers' with her. She smiled naughtily and asked, 'Here too?'

'Why not?' Danny whispered back.

'Okay,' Rivanah said. She took a small sip from his glass. He followed suit and they kissed letting the liquid merge.

'Cheers!' Danny said, breaking the kiss and gulping down the wine she had in her mouth.

'Cheers!' Rivanah repeated, conscious of the fact that the Stranger was privy to every word of their conversation.

'So, why this sudden dinner plan? Any more surprises coming up?' Danny said gazing into her eyes. Rivanah's guilt broke the gaze. She took another sip from his glass even though she had said she wouldn't drink.

'I'm a little worried about something.' She paused seeing Danny's expectant face. And then continued, 'There's a friend of mine . . .' she said, with her throat drying up every second, 'who loves her boyfriend a lot. Like, genuinely. But she had a slip.'

'Slip?'

'She cheated on him. Just once. Not wilfully, though. It just happened. She didn't intend to cheat on him, and in her heart she still loves her boyfriend. Only her boyfriend.' Rivanah stopped suddenly, realizing she was justifying this 'friend' of hers a little too much.

'Hmm, and whom did she cheat on him with?'

'Her roommate's boyfriend,' she said, looking at Danny who was lost in thought while sipping his wine.

'Actually, the roommate's boyfriend was an old friend of hers,' Rivanah corrected herself. Danny still didn't respond.

'I mean the roommate's boyfriend was this girl's ex,' Rivanah finally blurted out. Danny shot a sharp glance at her as if he had already judged this imaginary friend of hers.

'If it was her ex, then I'm sure it wasn't just a slip. Like, if I meet my ex and it ends up in a . . . wait a minute. Did you mean she simply kissed him when you said she slipped, or did she fuck her ex?'

'They . . .' She took yet another sip from Danny's glass and said, 'They fucked.'

'Whoa, then it obviously isn't a slip. By the way, are you sure you don't want to have wine?'

Rivanah shook her head and said, 'Why do you think that?'

'Because you are drinking all of mine,' Danny said in a lighter vein.

'Not that. Why do you think it was not a slip? How are you so sure?'

'You slip with strangers but you don't slip with people you already know. Especially your ex.'

Rivanah frowned. It didn't make sense to her. She probably didn't want it to make sense. All she wanted to hear from him was: it was just a slip, why bother? And since it didn't come the way she desired from Danny, Rivanah felt all the more frustrated.

'Anyway, what's up with this friend of yours?' Danny asked.

'She is in a fix whether to tell her present boyfriend about it or not.'

'Hmm. Okay.'

By then, the waiter laid out the sushi platter. But instead of the platter, Rivanah's eyes were on Danny.

He was about to say something when she cut him short saying, 'What do you reckon? What should the girl do? Tell her boyfriend everything?'

'I don't know. If it is not important, then she probably shouldn't,' he said, gobbling up a sushi.

'It's yum—' but before he could finish his sentence, she shut his lips with a kiss. He had finally said what she wanted to hear. There was no reason whatsoever for her to confess anything. Danny's opinion was, of course, more important and valuable to her than the Stranger's demand which now seemed all the more futile. The slip wasn't important for her so there was no reason why she should tell Danny about it. Period. She knew this from day one. It was the Stranger who had pushed her to believe otherwise. She took a bite of the sushi wondering if the Stranger had heard Danny's point of view. But he wouldn't know she wasn't going to comply with him. Doesn't matter what he said, he hadn't kept his part of the deal. Coming in front of her when she was in an inebriated state was a sheer breach. And now he would get in return exactly that—a breach. Danny took out his phone, stretched his hand and the two of them squeezed together beaming ear to ear for a selfie. Rivanah grabbed the phone from him to see how the selfie had come out. They looked happy together. No confession was bigger than the happiness that seemed to emanate from the selfie for her.

'What are you looking at?' Danny asked, taking the phone from her. Rivanah simply smiled and said, 'I love you.'

'I love you too.'

The waiter was back. 'Would you like to order your main course, sir?' he asked Danny.

'Certainly.'

'You order. I'll be back from the restroom,' Rivanah said.

'But what do you want to have?'

'I chose starters. You choose the main course for us,' she said with a heart-warming smile and headed towards the restroom.

In the restroom, Rivanah received a call from Sadhu Ram's number.

'Where are you?' Rivanah said the moment she picked up the call.

'Hello, Mini.'

Rivanah almost bit her own tongue.

'The first thing you will do after you step out of the restroom is confess,' the Stranger said.

'No, I won't. Didn't you hear? It is not important for Danny.'

'It is important for you, Mini.'

'No, it is not. Who are you to decide what's important for me and what's not?' Rivanah was surprised at the way she was talking to the Stranger. *But this is what is needed*, she told herself. This person was responsible for the life-threatening incidents in her life only weeks back, but she couldn't take it all lying down. A couple of seconds later she heard the line cut. She looked at her phone expecting another call but all that came was Danny's WhatsApp stating he was getting bored. Rivanah quickly stepped out. She was about to join Danny at the table when five men barged into the restaurant. She identified one of them. It was Sadhu Ram. She looked at the others. *Probably his men*, she thought, until she looked at the one who was right in front of Sadhu Ram. She knew this man too. It was Argho Chowdhury.

'We caught him red-handed with an ear piece,' Sadhu Ram said with a victorious smile.

17

Rivanah, Danny, Sadhu Ram along with his men and Argho were at the Bandra police station. The way the entire thing had played out reminded Rivanah of Abhiraj and how he was caught at Starbucks some time back. The difference being previously it wasn't the Stranger who was caught.

'So, it's all very simple: confess everything, or else we will do things our way,' Sadhu Ram said, oddly relaxed.

'Confess what?' Argho shouted. 'I don't know why I've been brought here! Rivanah, what nonsense is going on?'

'Talk to me, not to the girl,' said Sadhu Ram, holding Argho's chin up. He was handcuffed and made to sit on a chair in the middle of a cell, while Rivanah, Danny and the inspector in charge of the police station were standing in a circle around him.

'What were you doing at Bungalow 9?'

'I had a date.'

'With whom? Where's the girl?' Sadhu Ram took Argho's phone from his subordinate. They had confiscated it from him at the restaurant.

Argho looked at Sadhu Ram and said uncomfortably, 'I don't know her.'

Sadhu Ram smirked as if he was expecting it. 'That, I believe. You won't know her because there was no date. I have been following you for a week now, but haven't seen you with any girl.'

'You have been following me? For what?'

'Forget that and answer me first. Who is this girl you just mentioned?'

'We connected on Tinder,' Argho said. He was speaking softly now.

'Tinder? I know Tardeo but where is Tinder?' Sadhu Ram said, looking at his subordinates for clues.

'It is a dating app,' Rivanah spoke up. 'It is an app that you can download for free in your phone. You have to sign in through your Facebook account, after which you can find a match with prospective people.'

'I have to check your phone. What's the password?' Sadhu Ram gave the phone to Argho after unlocking the handcuffs. He made a pattern on the screen to unlock it. Sadhu Ram took the phone away and went to Rivanah. She tapped on it few times and opened Tinder. There were five matches.

'Which one?' Sadhu Ram asked Argho.

'Kanika Negi.'

'Does the name ring a bell?' Sadhu Ram asked Rivanah. Negative.

Sadhu Ram scrolled down and, along with Rivanah, read through the messages on the Tinder chat screen. There had been around fifty messages exchanged between Argho and Kanika. It was evident they didn't know each other and had casually decided to meet up at Bungalow 9 that night. That couldn't have been a coincidence; Rivanah was sure of it. The moment they reached the first message—a 'Hi' from Argho—a new message popped up right at that instant. Both Sadhu Ram and Rivanah read it and looked at each other with fright. The message read:

Argho is innocent. Mini is not.

The next instant, Kanika unmatched Argho from Tinder. And her profile wasn't live any more.

'Who is Mini?' Sadhu Ram asked.

'I am,' Rivanah said, her throat going dry.

'You are Mini?'

'It's her nickname,' Danny butted in.

It was clear now that Argho wasn't the Stranger. Or at least he wasn't alone in this.

'Why did the message say you are the culprit?' Sadhu Ram looked at Rivanah.

'I . . .' She glanced at Danny and said, 'I have no idea.'

'Hmm.' Sadhu Ram turned towards Argho and said, 'What about the difference in the kilometre reading on your bike?'

'What difference? I only use my bike sometimes, not every day.'

'I know you don't use it every day but—'

Sadhu Ram told him about how he had found there was a difference in the kilometre reading on his bike that particular day. As the two argued over the matter, Rivanah understood once and for all: Argho wasn't the Stranger. He was a pawn in an elaborate game. Just like she was. She couldn't help but feel astounded at how elaborate the game really was!

'What about the ear piece?' Sadhu Ram asked. Rivanah could tell even Sadhu Ram sounded frustrated now.

'That's my ear piece. Kanika asked me to put it on as a mark of identification.'

Argho took the phone from Rivanah and showed them the message where Kanika had written: *Put on an ear piece. I'll recognize you with it.* The same Kanika whose profile had been deactivated now.

'Madarchod!' Sadhu Ram shouted, stamping his foot on the ground. He simply couldn't take it that twice the Stranger had made a complete fool out of him. He apologized to Rivanah for the curse. Half an hour later, Sadhu Ram and the inspector on duty let Rivanah and Danny go. Argho was also allowed to leave as it was evident he was being set up.

'But you may have to come up to the station if summoned,' the inspector on duty said.

'Sure. I'm not guilty of anything, so why wouldn't I cooperate?' Argho said taking his phone from Sadhu Ram.

Outside, Rivanah and Danny were waiting for Argho. As he appeared, Rivanah apologized to him.

'As you already know there has been some confusion. I'm really sorry for this,' she said.

'I didn't know you had a police guy behind me! What is this all about?'

Rivanah felt pushed to tell him about his cousin Hiya's connection but held herself back at the last moment. By now it had become a long story. *Too long indeed*, she thought and said, 'Honestly Argho, even I'm yet to figure it out.'

'I completely fail to understand how I can be roped into something this serious about which I have no clue!'

Rivanah shot an embarrassing look at Danny so he could bail her out of the situation. He understood.

'We are sorry, Argho. It's just that even we have been misled. I hope you understand. Rivanah's intention wasn't to malign you in any way. It was all a misunderstanding. There's a stalker who is creating trouble. Probably the same person who connected with you via Tinder—Kanika Negi.'

Argho stood there looking around as if he still needed to be convinced.

'If the person wanted to frame me, then why would he or she message saying I'm innocent?' Argho argued.

Rivanah wanted to speak but didn't. It wasn't about Argho, she knew. It was about her. Only she knew the subtext of the last message from 'Kanika Negi'. Argho was just a tool to mislead her, corner her and make her do things which the Stranger wanted.

'I hope it gets sorted out for you fast,' Argho said looking at Rivanah. 'Whatever it is.'

'I hope so too.'

Argho took a cab and left. Danny climbed into his car. Rivanah excused herself and, taking a couple of steps away from the car, called her father.

'Baba, did Inspector Rajat Das get in touch with you?'

'No, what happened?'

'Nothing. I think we should take the complaint against Argho back.'

'How can you be so sure?'

'I am, Baba. Please take the complaint back.'

'Hmm. But if not Argho then who attacked you?'

'I don't know. Let them find the person if they can. But it wasn't Argho.'

'Okay, I will talk to Rajat.'

Rivanah talked to her mother for a minute and then joined Danny in the car. After a short distance, Danny stopped the car at a street corner.

'What happened?' Rivanah asked. She had just put on some music to distract herself. Danny switched it off. Their eyes met.

'Why didn't you tell me?' Danny asked. There was a sudden harshness in his tone. She knew why.

'I was about to Danny.'

'About to? When? I thought you'd planned the dinner for me. For *us*. I thought you had dressed up for me. But—surprise, surprise—it wasn't!' He now sounded cross. *And rightly so,* Rivanah thought.

'The dress, the look, it was all for you, Danny.'

'Shut up. Even the dress was bugged. You knew it. I didn't. Why?'

'It was just . . . just . . .' Rivanah couldn't think of anything to say. And with that, she knew she had given Danny enough reason to raise a finger at her. And at her love towards him.

'That's because you don't trust me.'

'It is nothing like that. Sadhu Ram asked me not to involve anybody.'

'Anybody? Okay, so after being in a relationship for more than a year now, I'm *anybody* to you. Great!' Danny started the engine and put the car on gear.

'I'm sorry, Danny.'

'Don't I-am-sorry me.'

Rivanah saw that Danny felt the same disgust she had felt every time Ekansh said sorry to her.

'I genuinely—'

'Rivanah, I will tell you this once.' Danny cut her short, glancing intently at her and continued, 'I don't like the fact that you hide things from me. If there's anything, just let me know. Share it with me. Anything at all, okay?'

Rivanah had to clear her throat mildly before nodding. When they reached their apartment, Danny climbed out of the car saying, 'Please lock the car before coming. You always seem to forget.' He was gone before she could say anything.

In the silence of the garage, Rivanah could feel the sting of Danny's words. Everything in her life was an irony. The one she loved first—Ekansh—had ditched her, the one who loved her next—Danny—was being kept in the dark by her. She reclined the car seat and shut her eyes, desperately wishing everything to be okay when she suddenly opened her eyes again. *Hello, Mini.* The entire car echoed with the two words. In a flash, she turned back and saw a small phone placed on the back seat. It had been connected to the car's Bluetooth. The Stranger had heard her entire conversation with Danny before he got out of the car. She quickly took the phone in her hand.

'You just awarded yourself a storm, Mini. Be ready now.'

Rivanah shut her lips so tight with fear that they turned white. Swallowing a lump, she said, 'No please, we can negotiate this, right?'

'I'm not in the mood to negotiate any more, Mini.' The line went dead. Rivanah saw a bike vroom past right in front of her car and out of the garage. She could neither see the number plate, nor the model, though she knew who it was. The one she knew nothing about.

18

That night, Rivanah tried her best to win Danny over, but he wouldn't warm up to her touches or her deliberate conversation-initiating queries. She knew she should have shared everything with him but it had all happened so quickly that she had decided to tell him later. She had been confident that he would be all ears. She wasn't expecting this cold shoulder. The way he reacted told her how less we know our partners. Living with them day in and day out, we create our own biased versions of them and start projecting our interpretations of the person on to their personality—which more often than not is far from reality. Like she would never know if Danny and Nitya had ever been close or not. Like Danny still didn't know Rivanah had things hidden from him. Rivanah wanted to discuss this with someone, but she was sure it couldn't be the Stranger. *He may have shown her glimpses of his good soul, but overall he was a sadist*, Rivanah concluded. But then . . . who else could she talk to?

While going to the office the next day, Rivanah tapped ten digits on her phone and then pressed on the call button. She had deleted Ekansh's number but she remembered it by heart.

'Hi Rivanah. I knew you would call,' Ekansh said, picking up the call almost immediately. *Does he really mean what he said? He knew? Does Ekansh know me more than Danny does?* Rivanah brushed aside these thoughts and said, 'Ekansh, I want to ask you something. But promise me that you will answer to the point.'

'I promise,' he said after a pause.

'If Tista was alive, would you have told her about what happened between us that evening?'

'Look, Rivanah, we have . . .'

'Just answer the question, Ekansh,' Rivanah said and added softly, 'Please . . .'

She could hear him breathing.

'No, I wouldn't have told her.'

Rivanah sighed. She needed this reassurance to validate what she was doing with Danny. She told herself that anyone in love would have done the same thing. Sometimes, lies are the only way to keep a relationship running like a well-oiled machine.

'Thanks,' she said and hung up before Ekansh could say anything else. She thought he would call her back but he didn't. *He probably knew*, Rivanah wondered, *that she would herself call him when needed—the way she did minutes ago.*

In office, there were a few awkward glances exchanged between Rivanah and Argho, but neither said anything. He was Hiya's cousin, but till now he had showed no inclination whatsoever in trying to know if anything had happened between Hiya and Rivanah. He would have told Sadhu Ram during the interrogation in case he knew something. Or was he too smart for the police? Rivanah tried to forget the last thought.

For most of the day, Rivanah kept sending emotional messages to Danny but there was no response from him. In the end, she thought she would resolve it the way most couple fights get resolved: with time, by doing nothing about it at the moment. But she was in for a surprise. An hour before her work was about to get over, she got a gift pack from the security. There was no name on it. She tore open the gift wrap to reveal a small box. She unlocked it and found two pearl earrings along with a note saying: *Game for a fresh start?—D.*

She immediately called Danny up. He answered on the third ring.

'Danny, you dog, I'm going to kill you,' she said and heard him laugh. 'Stop laughing. This isn't funny. I have been messaging you all day like a moron.'

'Serves you right,' Danny said, with a hint of amusement in his voice.

'Really? Meet me tonight and I'll show you what suits you!'

'Is that a promise?'

'Like hell it is.'

'I shall be waiting.'

'You better.'

'Love you loads.'

'Love you back. When are you reaching home today?'

'Latest by eight. And you?'

'Should be there by nine.'

'Great.'

Rivanah then Googled 'best sexual surprises for boyfriend' on her desktop. A series of links appeared but just as she was about to open one, a beep on her phone stopped her. It was a WhatsApp message. The message was in the form of an image. The image was a Google map pinning her office as 'Address A'. A blue line from this point led to a point somewhere in Kalyan which was in the outskirts of Mumbai. The end pin was labelled, to her utter shock, 'Hiya Chowdhury'. She maximized the image on her phone. The message was obvious: Hiya, or some link to her, was in Kalyan. And Kalyan was a good two hours away from where Rivanah was at the moment. She quickly calculated: she had four hours before she had to reach her flat, just in time for Danny. Or should she go there with Danny? But what if that irks the Stranger and she misses out on the vital information on Hiya? Once again it was a catch-22 situation for Rivanah. There was no other friend whom she could request to follow her secretly, just in case there was danger. Ekansh's name crossed her mind but she wasn't sure. Only a few seconds later, she dialled Danny's number on an impulse.

'Hey baby, I'll be home by nine. Some work has come up. I'll call you the moment I'm done.'

'In office itself?'

'No.' She swallowed a lump. 'But somewhere nearby.' *If she said Kalyan, there can't be any excuse for her to be there at this hour,* she thought. Yet another lie. *But this would be the last,* she promised herself.

'Just call me once around nine,' she said, sounding pensive.

'Why?'

'I'll wrap it up quickly then,' she said, keeping the real reason from him. Just in case something happened, someone should have the right doubt at the right time.

'All right. I'll call you at nine,' Danny said.

'Thanks. Muah. Love you.'

Rivanah took a cab to Andheri railway station, took the metro till Ghatkopar and then a local train from the central line to reach Kalyan. Exhaustion made her doze off in the train itself. She was woken up by a fellow passenger when Kalyan—the last station on the line—arrived. Little did she know that someone was following her.

Once she came out of the rather busy Kalyan railway station, she took a cab without knowing where to go. She glanced at the image of the map once and told the cab driver she would guide him to the destination. Half a minute later, the person following her also hailed a cab and asked the driver to follow hers.

After about twenty five minutes, Rivanah reached the spot marked on the map. From inside the cab she tried to look out. There was nothing around. She opened the car's door and stepped out. She had no idea where she was. She tried to extract her location via Google but realized her mobile Internet wasn't working.

'Madam, rukna hai ya jaun?' the cab driver popped his head out of the window and asked. She knew there wasn't any chance of getting public transport in such a place and—her eyes fell on an ATM a few metres away. Strangely, the light inside the ATM was flickering.

'Madam?' the driver egged on.

Rivanah quickly took out her purse. To her surprise, she was short of the fare. In fact, all she had was a ten rupee note. She frowned, not remembering how much she was carrying. She told the driver she would need to take money out of the ATM, realizing this could well be part of the plan. *Was the clue to Hiya inside the ATM? Was the flickering of light a ploy to attract my attention? Did someone empty my wallet when I dozed off in the train so that I have no option but to use the ATM?*

'Bhaiya, main ek minute mein aati hun. Paise nikalne hai,' she told the cab driver, who made a face. Rivanah proceeded towards the ATM. Another cab had stopped at some distance behind her. The person following her stepped out of the cab and noticed her going towards the ATM. The person waited for her to enter the ATM.

Rivanah went close to the ATM entrance and tried to look through the glass door. There was nobody inside, and the lights were still flickering. She gently pushed the door open, still looking around, and slowly stepped inside. Why would the Stranger call her to such a place with Hiya marked on the map? *There has to be something to it*, she wondered, and glanced at the ATM screen. It was out of order. She sensed something was wrong. Just like the Planchette idea, this too seemed like a mistake.

You awarded yourself a storm . . . the Stranger's words came rushing to her. *Shit, shit, shit. Why the hell did I come here!* Rivanah thought, feeling anxious, and immediately turned around to leave. She paused, hearing her name being called out. It was a male voice. She froze. Was it the Stranger? But the voice was very familiar.

'Rivanah!' the voice called out again. She suddenly felt energy gushing to her feet as she turned around in a flash to see Ekansh.

'What are you doing here?' Rivanah looked to his right where there was a tiny room for the security guard. He was probably inside the room when she came in.

'I was waiting for you,' he said.

'For me? Why?' Looking at him, she felt scared like never before. Somehow he didn't seem like himself.

'You said you know how to connect to Tista,' he blabbered, as if he was under some spell.

'I did? What nonsense are you talking? How did I communicate with you?' She almost knew the answer.

'Through messages,' he said confused, and showed her his phone. Rivanah read the messages:

Hi Ekansh, I know of a way of communicating with Tista. Don't call me or message me back. If you are interested then just meet me at 7.30 at this address . . .

She didn't read the rest. It was yet again a case of SIM card duplication. The ease with which the Stranger duplicated SIM cards told Rivanah how dangerous technology was and how fatal its impact could be if in wrong hands. It was clear the Stranger was up to some game once again by calling Ekansh and her at the same spot, but why? She wanted to rush back home, to Danny. *Nothing was going to be revealed to me about Hiya. It is all a joke, a sick joke which the Stranger has been playing on me since my arrival in Mumbai.* Rivanah turned towards the door without saying anything to Ekansh. He held her hand. She turned to glance at him and said, 'Leave me, Ekansh, and go home. It wasn't me messaging you.'

'What do you mean?' His grip turned tighter. She had neither the time nor the intention to clarify anything.

'Someone was just messing with you. Chuck it and go.' It was the best excuse she could come up with. She again turned around to leave but he pulled her towards him. They came dangerously close, with Ekansh still gripping her hand while placing the other hand around her waist to hold her tight.

'What do you think of yourself, Rivanah?' Ekansh asked. His grip was hurting her as he continued, 'You can call me anytime, cut the phone line without saying anything, tell Tista about us, call me to a secluded ATM in the name of Tista, and then say it was all a joke? I won't allow you to treat me as if I'm some piece of shit.' The strength with which he held her not only hurt Rivanah but surprised her as well.

'Ekansh, it wasn't me. It's someone who is playing with me. Now leave me.'

'Who is it?'

'I don't know.'

'Just like you didn't know who told Tista the truth, right?'

'Shut up and leave me,' she said, trying to release herself from his grip.

Just outside the ATM, the person who had been following Rivanah to Kalyan station and then to the ATM pushed open the door. It was Danny.

Danny first looked at Rivanah, then at Ekansh, and then the way he was holding her. Ekansh let go of Rivanah. She was too dumbstruck to speak.

'I was outside your office when you called me. I kept telling myself that you love me too much to lie to me. Especially after we had both decided you won't hide anything from me.' Danny sighed and added, 'I tried to make you as comfortable as I could but still this sluttish behaviour—why? You could have just told me you are done with me,' Danny said, looking acutely hurt. It was evident he had misinterpreted the entire scene. But the word 'sluttish' stabbed Rivanah deeply. This name-calling was the last thing Rivanah expected from Danny.

'I think I should leave,' Ekansh mumbled awkwardly. He looked at Rivanah. Whatever anger his eyes were carrying against her a moment back suddenly changed into sympathy. Neither Rivanah nor Danny cared to look at him. As Ekansh stepped outside and shut the door, Rivanah asked in an injured tone, 'Why would you call me a slut, Danny? That too in front of Ekansh?'

'I didn't call you a slut. I just said your behaviour is that of a slut. Ask yourself why I said that. If you were not a slut, you wouldn't have lied to me to be here with your ex. God knows how many more times you guys have been together.'

'Who said I lied to you? I myself didn't know Ekansh was supposed to be here.'

'Yeah sure, like I'm going to believe you,' Danny said, without caring to look at her as he talked.

'You have to, because it's the truth. I came here because I was sent this,' Rivanah tapped her phone to show him the Google map image the stranger had sent her. He looked at it and then said, 'Okay. Look into my eyes and answer two questions.'

'Ask me anything.' Rivanah knew she was going to cry any moment now.

'Were you with Ekansh as the message claimed the night I came to your office?'

It took her some time but she nodded. Danny swallowed hard.

'But that's because ....' she started.

'Don't explain,' he said and continued to look straight into her eyes, 'Is there anything that you think I should know as far as you and Ekansh are concerned?'

Rivanah looked down.

'Look at me, goddamnit!' he shouted.

Rivanah slowly lifted her head up and then nodded. 'What is it?'

She was crying now as she spoke, 'I just can't tell you.' But she didn't have to, for Danny knew: that she and Ekansh were still in a relationship.

'Is it what I think it is?'

'I simply can't tell you about it,' Rivanah said, feeling shame and humiliation squeeze all the pain out of her core.

'So let me rephrase. It wasn't sluttish behaviour. You are a slut. That's what it is,' Danny said in a concluding tone.

'Please don't say that, Danny. I love you.'

'Shut the fuck up.'

'You just can't come here, interpret everything wrongly and call me names, Danny. You have to listen to me. Your inference isn't the whole story.'

'I. Don't. Care. Any more,' he said, locking his jaws.

Rivanah felt a sudden anger honking hard within her. But she didn't know what she was angry about: the fact that she didn't tell Danny about the matter or the fact that his reaction was exactly how she thought any man would react. *Any man!* If this was any man's reaction, then what did Danny mean when he said he loved her? Any man would have labelled her a slut misinterpreting the scene or the truth which she nested within her—but not the one who loved her, for that man would have actually understood it was indeed a slip and respected the fact that she too had the right to explain. *In an ideal world, that is.* If she was a slut, then she would have continued fucking Ekansh, fucking every other man she came across without feeling guilty about it. But her love for Danny was exactly why she couldn't confess to him in the first place. But by saying she was a slut, did Danny think he had washed his hands off the relationship, off her?

'So you are saying there's nothing for me to react to, right?' Danny said.

'Right.' Rivanah said it more out of anger than anything else. She knew he had the right to react but she had a problem with the way he was reacting—like someone who never knew her.

'If you really think there's nothing for me to react, then why don't you tell me the truth yourself?' Danny asked.

I don't mind your reaction, Danny. I just don't get how you have already decided what my intention was and given it a name, she thought, but couldn't say it aloud. *Anybody would reach conclusions about you in no time, but when your closest one too does it, then what's left to say? Conclusions are made very swiftly, but to break them one needs time*, she thought. And Danny didn't seem to be in the mood to give her time.

There was silence as Danny waited for her to speak. She knew whatever she said now would be twisted by him, turned into an arrow and darted right back at her.

'You continue to be quiet and still don't want me to react the way I'm doing. Awesome!' Danny said.

As he was about to leave, Rivanah blurted out, 'Ekansh and I slept with each other some time back.'

Danny stood frozen for a few seconds and then turned around to look at her. 'Were we together then?'

Rivanah nodded like a programmed machine and hung her head in shame. She looked up when she heard a loud bang. Danny had smashed his hand on the ATM door creating a crack in the glass. She immediately took his hand in hers to check the extent of the injury.

'Stay. Away,' he said pushing her back. His touch had never felt so condescending.

'Remember how you walked out on me because of Nitya?' Danny asked, facing away from her. He then turned around and, looking straight at her, said, 'I think it is time to walk out again. Just that, this time, it will be me walking out on you.'

'Why aren't you listening to me?' Her frustration was evident in her tone. 'It is not what it sounds like.'

'You just said you fucked your ex when we were in a relationship. To me, it sounds pretty simple.'

'It just happened, Danny. It. Just. Happened. I have avoided Ekansh since then.'

'I saw a minute back how much you guys have avoided each other. Meeting in a secluded ATM after you told me you had some office work? I don't know what you call it, but for me this is sluttish behaviour.'

'Please don't say that. Had I been a slut, I would have continued to sleep with Ekansh. But I never did that.'

'And you think that, after what I saw here and whatever you confessed, I'm going to believe you? Do you understand, Rivanah, I can't turn a blind eye to your acts any more?'

Who is this Danny? Rivanah wondered. *How can the person I love so dearly behave like a stranger? One sight of me with Ekansh, and Danny has already judged me? Can one be so blinded by love?*

'I love you, Danny. Only you. Why aren't you getting it?' Rivanah blurted out.

Danny smirked and said, 'That's what I thought too. And would have continued to think all my life, had I not been led to this place.'

'The one who led you to this place led me here as well,' she said.

'That changes nothing.'

Rivanah mentally cursed the Stranger for having stirred this and said aloud, 'Let's just go home, sit down and talk it out. I can explain everything. Then I'm sure you will understand.'

'I'm sorry, but I can't be associated with a lying whore,' Danny said and turned to leave. He knew the last part was little too much but he didn't care. If this was too much, then what was that she confessed? A raging frown appeared on Rivanah's face. On an impulse, she followed him.

'You really want to know what a whore is, Danny?' Rivanah shouted. This was the first time she had raised her voice this high in front of someone she loved.

'I'll show you and then you can walk out on me,' Rivanah said, her entire body shaking. She saw Ekansh in the distance, perhaps waiting for a cab. She crossed Danny and called out to Ekansh. Ekansh was taken aback seeing Rivanah come up to him.

Before Ekansh could speak, Rivanah grabbed him by his collar, pressed her lips against his and with one hand clicked a picture of them kissing. She broke the kiss the next second and sent the picture to Danny on WhatsApp. Looking towards Danny, who was still beside the ATM, she shouted, 'Check your phone, Danny, to know what a real whore is like.' Rivanah smashed her phone on the ground. It broke into pieces but it wasn't the only thing that broke.

'Rivanah!' Ekansh called out. She turned and said, 'Don't you follow me.' And walked out of his sight.

She found a cab at a distance and told the driver to take her to Dahisar.

It was the same area where she had taught Mini's Magic 10. The destination didn't matter to her. All she wanted was to cry alone. It was already dark when she reached the place three hours later. Looking around, the only lonely spot she could see was the skywalk. She climbed the stairs and took the empty bench under a light, feeling progressively suicidal. *What was left?* she asked herself. *A big nothing. How do you build anything from that big nothing and still call it life?* Rivanah cried.

It was over with Ekansh long ago, and now it was over with Danny too. Next time it won't be 'falling' in love for her. From here on, it would be suffering in love. But did she have the energy to suffer in love again? She wiped her tears and tried to breathe, but her nose was slightly blocked. Sitting under one of the lamp posts, she thought she heard footsteps coming towards her. She peered into the darkness but didn't see anybody. She sighed and was about to bury her face in her hands again when she heard a voice say, 'Hello, Mini.'

Rivanah slowly looked up—in anticipation. And fear. And disgust.

19

For a split second, Rivanah thought she had simply imagined the voice, before she noticed the tips of someone's shoes at the edge of the light. The light overhead did not fall on his face, and most of him was shrouded in darkness, but it didn't take her long to guess who this someone could be.

'Is that you?' Rivanah said aloud. Her voice was brittle.

The response came after few seconds.

'Yes, Mini.'

Her eyes were transfixed on the shining black tips of the shoes. Rivanah stood up, expecting the Stranger to take a step back. But he didn't. Rivanah took a step towards him. He was still. Slowly, she began inching towards the Stranger. With every step, her heart beat faster. And every beat felt heavy with anxiety. When she stood close to him, she could smell his deodorant— Just Different from Hugo Boss. *It is indeed him!* But his face and body remained shrouded in darkness. Rivanah took the final few steps and stood only inches away from the tips of the shoes. Breathing had become difficult. The fact that the Stranger hadn't moved told her he wanted her to unmask him. She was about to reach out when two hands shot out and, before Rivanah could understand what was happening, she was turned around forcefully and blindfolded. Rivanah felt him tightening the blindfold. Slowly, the Stranger pulled her into the darkness, away from the sight of any pedestrian.

'I . . .' Rivanah started, but she felt a finger on her lips and a whisper right next to her left ear, 'Ssshhh.' She felt a little aroused even in her state of emotional distress.

'Pain is a seed, Mini. And it often grows into a tree we call strength. A seed of strength has been sown in you today, Mini. You have no idea how emotionally stable a tree this will become,' the Stranger whispered. His breath tickled her ear as she allowed this idea to take root in her. She could feel his cotton shirt as she grabbed it tight with both hands. Not able to hold herself back any more, she buried her face in the Stranger's chest and cried her heart out. She knew it would be useless to try to get rid of the blindfold.

'I never wanted to tell Danny the truth because the incident didn't compromise my love for him. Please say you know this. Please . . .'

'I know, Mini,' the Stranger whispered back.

'Then why did you do this to me? Why did you lead Ekansh, me and Danny to the ATM today? This is an irreparable damage. I don't think Danny will ever understand why I couldn't confess. It was only out of love.'

'I know Danny will never understand it.'

Rivanah frowned. She tried to touch the Stranger's face but he wouldn't let her.

'You have to tell me why you did this to me!' she said.

'First, you tell me, Mini, what's love if it doesn't let you give your loved one some time to explain? If it stands like a wall between you and your beloved? There are already a lot of walls in a relationship, Mini. What's rare is a freeway for trust.'

Rivanah listened hard as the Stranger continued, 'This confession of yours wasn't a test for you, Mini, it was a test of Danny's love. He is hurt not because you didn't confess to him but because you supposedly cheated on him. He doesn't want to give you a chance to explain. It's difficult to be with someone who prefers his own assumptions to his partner's reality.'

Rivanah wasn't sure what she felt at that moment.

'Ekansh ditched me, Danny didn't understand me. And I loved both with all my heart. What else can I do apart from loving someone honestly? I have tried the best I could, and it didn't work. What else remains for me to give anyone? I somehow managed to come to terms with Ekansh's betrayal but this . . . how will I be able to forget this scar, this hurt that Danny has given me by not understanding me?'

'To forget a hurt, Mini, we subconsciously seek a bigger and deeper hurt. Happiness is a vacation. Hurt is our home.'

'I was so confident nothing will go wrong between Danny and me.' She choked. For the first time, she felt the Stranger's hand caressing her back. Somehow she couldn't blame the Stranger any more for stirring the storm he did in the ATM, because otherwise she would have continued to live a lie.

'You will have to learn to let go, Mini. Life's not about what you have. It's about how much and how easily you let go of what you have.'

There were footsteps. The Stranger placed one hand on Rivanah's mouth, the other behind her back, and drew her closer to his chest. She could hear his heartbeat. It sounded normal. Hers definitely was not. The embrace calmed her. And he was . . . she lifted her head and felt his breath on her face. As she tasted her own tears, her lips parted. She didn't know whether the Stranger was looking at her—she wished he was. But when she felt a thumb caressing her lips, she was sure he was looking at her. She didn't know which was scarier: the comfort she was feeling in the arms of a stranger or a stranger making her this comfortable. But she knew whichever of the two it was, it was the most compelling fear she had ever felt.

Two young boys walked past them, chatting cheerfully, not noticing them in the dark. Once their voices became faint, the Stranger slowly released Rivanah from his grip. They stood a few inches apart.

'Why do you keep breaking me and then making me at the same time?'

The Stranger didn't respond immediately. Rivanah thought he was gone. She stretched her hand and relaxed when she felt him.

'That's what true love is, isn't it?' the Stranger asked. 'Helping the other person grow by constantly breaking and making them at the same time? Not the way you want them to be but the way they ought to be.'

'Do you mean you love—' Rivanah felt a finger on her lips before she could finish.

'That's not important, Mini. What is important is why you forgot about Hiya all of a sudden after you visited Mr Dutta in Kolkata? Ask yourself that. And get an answer soon. Time is running out.'

'But you won't kill me, right?'

There was no response. She couldn't touch him any more with her hands. Rivanah quickly opened her blindfold. She looked around and found herself all alone on the skywalk. Why did she forget about Hiya after visiting Mr Dutta? Did she really visit Mr Dutta? Wasn't it supposed to be a dream? Her parents had confirmed it for her. The Stranger must be kidding.

20

Rivanah had little choice but to return to the flat she shared with Danny. She used the spare key to unlock it. She was sure she would find him inside and had no clue how to handle the situation. But instead of Danny, she found a Post-it note on the refrigerator. It read:

I know it sounds rude but you haven't left me with any other option. Please leave by tomorrow. Thanks.

It wasn't just rude. It was formal. Way too formal. And that was more hurtful. Two people claiming to be in love until few hours back now behaving like strangers. Rivanah threw the note in the dustbin and went to the bedroom. By then she had realized Danny wasn't home. He wouldn't be till the next day—till she left. In only a few hours she had become an emotional disease he couldn't bear to see. She switched on the night lamp in the bedroom and looked at the nicely made bed. They had made love on the bed time and again, whispering promises to each other and confessing their love. What were those promises and confessions? Just a momentary illusion squeezed out by the hunger of the body? Rivanah sat on the bed and caressed the bed sheet. The place which once had the fragrance of their togetherness would have the stain of her tears tomorrow. But would the stains be prominent enough to be noticed by Danny? Rivanah doubted it as a teardrop fell on the bed sheet. She lay down on the bed, clutching the bed sheet tight, and quietly cried her way to sleep.

Rivanah woke up in the morning, took a little more than an hour to pack all her stuff except for the ones gifted to her by Danny and pasted a blank note on the refrigerator. She didn't have anything to say and hoped Danny would understand. She had finally understood men. They would demand chance after chance when they were at fault but wouldn't give a woman any chance—it didn't matter if she was at fault or not. Their straying is always accidental but a woman's straying is part of her personality. Most importantly, a man's mistake is a woman's sin.

There was a surprise waiting for her in front of the main door. Her mobile phone. The one she had smashed to the ground the previous evening. She picked it up trying to guess who could have kept it there. There was no damage to it. Did the Stranger buy her a new phone, same model? Switching it on she realized it was her phone; all repaired.

Initially Rivanah thought she'd go to Meghna's place, dump her stuff and head to office but decided against it midway. She couldn't trouble her every time she was in a spot. Especially since Rivanah had never bothered to keep in touch with her. The kind of spite she had felt seeing Riju with Meghna last time eventually steered her mind off. With no clue where to go at such short notice, Rivanah went to the office with her luggage. When her colleagues enquired about the reason for such a sudden shift, she made up excuses.

Rivanah thought she could find temporary accommodation with the colleagues she was close to, but they all gave some excuse or other. She talked with two or three brokers for a rented place, but nothing was available immediately. In the end she thought of putting up at a hotel near her office until she found a flat. She booked a room. Rivanah was surprised—she wasn't as disarrayed as she thought she would be. She even faked a perfectly normal tone while talking to her mother. The Rivanah who had come to Mumbai wouldn't have been able to be so composed and practical after a break-up. It was the Rivanah who had stayed in Mumbai and fought whatever had come her way.

In the evening, as she dragged her luggage into the office elevator on her way out and pressed the ground floor button, a foot stopped the door from closing. She looked up to see Nivan.

'Hey,' he said and entered the elevator.

'Hey.' Rivanah was glad to see him. Nivan glanced at her luggage and said, 'Did you just rob our office?'

Rivanah smiled and replied, 'House issues. Need to find a place ASAP.'

'Oh. Didn't the landlord give you any notice?'

Rivanah's smile went dry as she said, 'Not really.'

'That's quite indecent on his part.'

Rivanah nodded in agreement. The elevator door opened on the ground floor. 'See you,' Nivan said and stepped out of the elevator before she could reply. She dragged her luggage out and went out of her office building to fetch an autorickshaw. Had it not been for her luggage, she could have walked the distance. To her dismay, no auto was ready to take her to the hotel such a short distance away. A pitch-black BMW came to halt right in front of her. Rivanah didn't notice who was inside it until the window rolled down. It was Nivan. And her stupid smile was back.

'Where are you going to put up tonight?' Nivan asked trying to lean sideways away from the steering wheel in order to make eye contact.

'Hotel Hometel. It's very close—'

'I know where Hometel is,' he cut her short. 'But I think I've a permanent solution for you.'

'You do? I'm listening.'

'I own an empty flat right opposite the one I live in. You can stay there if it is okay with you.'

'Thanks, but I think it would be a problem for you.'

'Not really. I'm anyway thinking of letting the flat out. Might as well start with you.'

So it's not charity, Rivanah thought, and said, 'In that case, I don't mind.'

Nivan got out of the car and helped her put the luggage in the boot. Rivanah cast furtive glances at Nivan all through their ride, but not once did she see him return any. She would have loved it if he had asked her something. That would have given her the licence to ask him some as well without sounding like a probing psycho.

Nivan lived in a posh locality near the Lokhandwala market in Andheri West. Five minutes from Krishna Towers where she lived with Danny. *Used to live with Danny*, she corrected herself. Once inside the society premises, she knew she wouldn't be able to afford the rent there. The Residency Enclave was visibly an upscale area. She thought it'd be rude if she refused outright since Nivan was concerned enough to have driven her to the place.

He lived on the sixteenth floor. Flat number 1603. He pressed the doorbell and they exchanged a formal smile.

The door was opened by an old female servant. She took Nivan's laptop bag as a Labrador rushed towards him, wagging its tail.

'Meet Xeno,' Nivan told Rivanah.

'Say hello to . . .' Nivan told Xeno, caressing him, and then turned to Rivanah saying, 'It's Rivanah, right?'

'Yes.'

'Say hi to Rivanah,' Nivan spoke into Xeno's ears.

'Niv!' A lady called out from one of the rooms inside.

'Please be comfortable, and give me a minute,' Nivan told Rivanah and went in as Xeno sniffed her. She patted its head lovingly and walked to the huge white sofa and sat down. Xeno too sat down right beside her feet on the Kashmiri carpet. The servant who had opened the door came with a glass of water. While sipping the water, a tiny part of her was praying that the woman who called Nivan inside was his mother. Or aunt. Or whoever except . . . her eyes fell on a lot of photographs, mostly of Nivan and another girl. But before she could take a closer look at the pictures, Nivan came out into the drawing room.

'Let's go,' he said and went towards the main door. Rivanah kept her glass on the tray on the centre table. As she followed Nivan, Xeno followed her.

It was flat no. 1604, right opposite his, as Nivan had said. Rivanah realized there was no nameplate on the front door as she saw him switch on the lights. He asked Rivanah to follow him inside. She did along with Xeno.

It was a well-furnished flat. There was a little dust in the air, which told Rivanah it must have been closed for some time, but it was a cosy place nonetheless. Nivan went to a corner and pressed a button. Slowly the curtains which Rivanah had been mistaking for wallpaper drew themselves to one side bringing alive a breathtaking view of the Versova beach. Rivanah's jaw fell open as she went close to the glass wall. She could see the evening horizon in the distance as the sun almost set in its lap. It was almost a dream flat for her but soon reality set in. She couldn't afford such a place.

'Give me eighteen thousand a month for this, and it's all yours. No brokerage. No advance,' she heard Nivan say. Rivanah immediately turned around to look at him.

'Okay. How many tenants will you allow?' she asked.

'It's all yours. No sharing business.'

A smile of disbelief escaped her. 'You must be kidding?' Rivanah said.

'No, I'm not,' Nivan said kneeling down to caress Xeno.

'This flat's rent, considering the locality, should be around eighty thousand a month. And you are asking me to pay eighteen with no other roommates? That has to be a joke.'

'What you mentioned is the market rate. But the rent is decided by someone else.'

'Someone else? Who?'

'The landlady.'

'Oh, I thought you owned the place.'

'I own the place but someone else rules it,' Nivan said with a faint smirk.

'May I know who that landlady is?'

'You'll get to know soon. I hope you liked the place though.'

'I love it. And I can't thank you enough, sir.'

'Call me Nivan. And we'll make an agreement by noon tomorrow.'

Rivanah smiled and said, 'Thanks, Nivan.'

'Don't mention it. You can have a look at the entire flat first.'

'Sure,' Rivanah said and went in. It was a fully furnished two-bedroom flat. *Only a blind person can say no to this one*, Rivanah thought, and paused at the bedroom entrance seeing something.

'All good?' Nivan startled Rivanah.

'A sketch stand?' Rivanah said, looking at the sketch stand in the bedroom.

'It belongs to the one who stayed in this flat before you. Been some time. I didn't want to throw it away, actually. After all, it's art and I appreciate it.'

Rivanah walked up to the sketch stand. There were sheets on it. The first sketch was of a woman's face.

'I can get this removed if it's too much of a bother,' Nivan offered.

'Let it be,' Rivanah said as she touched the sheet. She neither knew nor remembered that it was her own sketch of Hiya Chowdhury's face. 'It's lovely,' Rivanah added.

21

Rivanah ordered from Subway that night. She was so tired because of the constant shuttling that she had no strength to cook. Only when the sub and diet Coke arrived did it strike her that she had not eaten a morsel in the last twenty-four hours. Post dinner, she called up her mother. Since her Kolkata trip, the frequency of her mother's calls had increased as well. After the attack, she understood their concern. The police hadn't been able to find a lead. Though she talked to her mother for almost half an hour, she didn't say a word about what had happened between Danny and her. She could well imagine her father's reaction once he knew: *I told you so!* And never again would she be able to convince him about her choice in the future—*if* she has a choice in the future. Lying down in bed, Rivanah's eyes fell on the sketch stand next to her with the face of a girl. Rivanah had brought her own sketch stand when she had left Danny's place, but had instructed the guard to discard it since she wouldn't need it. She had no idea what it was doing at Danny's house in the first place—she definitely couldn't remember sketching anything. But Danny had said she was the one who had sketched those faces. And now, lying on the bed gaping at the sketch, she felt there was something familiar about it. But what was it? The Stranger's last question to her before he disappeared popped up in her mind: *Why did you forget about Hiya after meeting Mr Dutta?* Why would her parents deny something which had happened for real? Or was the Stranger up to some mind games again? Rivanah immediately picked up her phone and called her mother. It was 10.30 p.m. She didn't care that they might be asleep.

'Mumma?'

'Mini? Is everything all right?' her mother asked, sounding anxious.

'Yes, all is fine. Tell me, Mumma, did I ever sketch before?' Rivanah asked.

There was silence.

'Mumma?'

'Mini?' Her father came on the line.

'Baba? Where's Mumma? What happened?'

'That's what I want to know. What happened? Why are you asking about sketching at this odd hour?' Her father sounded as anxious as her mother.

'Everything is fine. I just wanted to know if I sketched before or not.'

'Yes, you used to sketch. But you left that hobby long back.'

Long back? 'Hmm. Okay. Goodnight, Baba.'

'Are you sure everything is okay, Mini?'

'Yes. Goodnight, Baba.'

'Goodnight, Mini,' her father said, still sounding concerned.

Rivanah kept staring at the sketch and then shut her eyes to sleep.

The next morning, before going to office, Nivan's agent had come to take her signature on the rental agreement. Rivanah didn't see Nivan leaving for office around the time she did, though she secretly wished he had. His presence—she had realized in the car with him the other day—made her disconnect with the mess her life was. The sight of him was a sweet escape. But one thing she had promised herself: even if she felt attracted to him, she wouldn't fall for him. In fact, she wouldn't fall for any man again. After two failed relationships, Rivanah didn't want to take a chance. Not so soon. Not ever, if possible.

In the office, Rivanah was surprised to know that she and Nivan had become a couple overnight for most of her teammates.

'Don't lie! Rohit saw you guys together. Didn't he give you a lift yesterday?' asked one.

'Yeah, but—'

'How is he in bed?' asked another inquisitive co-worker.

'Shut up! I needed a place to stay so—'

'OMG! You are staying with Nivan?' said another colleague almost having a heart attack.

'No! Someplace close to his.' Rivanah intentionally lied to avoid any further questions.

'Did you find out anything about him?' Rivanah understood she wasn't the only one crushing on Nivan. He was quite a hit with the office females. Twice while fetching hot cappuccino for herself, Rivanah came across Nivan, but his body language was so formal that she wondered if he was the same person who had given her a lift and lent out his flat at half the market rate.

During the day, whenever her phone buzzed with a message, Rivanah thought it would be Danny, but it never was. When she checked her WhatsApp during lunch, she saw Danny's display picture wasn't visible to her. He must have deleted her number. *So easily?* It scared her. Are relationships that brittle? Or are humans that unpredictable? Rivanah remembered how her cousin Meghna and Aadil broke up after almost a decade of being together. The worst part of such an experience is that it no longer lets you be in control of your own life, blinding you in the process.

She deleted Danny's number. A supposed intimate connection between two human beings was finally over with one tap of a finger on a mechanical device.

In the evening, Rivanah went straight to her flat, feeling mentally exhausted. The moment she unlocked the door, a pleasant smell hit her. She followed it to the dining table where she saw a bowl covered with a plate.

It was payesh. And this one smelt exactly the way her mother used to make it. Rivanah scooped out some with her index finger, and licked it, relishing the taste. *But who kept it here?*

Rivanah picked up the bowl and went to Nivan's door and rang the doorbell. The servant opened the door.

'Hi, I wanted to know if you kept this inside the flat,' Rivanah said.

The female servant nodded and gestured her to come inside.

'No, I'm fine. Just wanted to know if it was you. Did you prepare it?'

The servant suddenly grabbed her hand and tried to pull her inside the flat. It didn't take much time to understand that she was dumb. She gestured Rivanah to sit down, closed the main door, and scampered inside. Xeno came running towards Rivanah, wagging its tail. The servant came into the drawing room pushing a wheelchair on which sat a pristine-looking girl. She was smiling at Rivanah. *Is she the one who called Nivan the other day from the bedroom?* Rivanah wondered.

'Hi,' the girl said as the servant brought her close to Rivanah.

'Hi. I'm Rivanah Bannerjee. I stay—'

'I know. I'm Advika,' the girl interrupted. Her words came out slurry.

And what's your relation with Nivan? Rivanah thought, but said, 'Nice to meet you,' extending her right hand.

Instead of the right, Advika lifted her left hand saying, 'I'm sorry, Rivanah, my right side doesn't function.'

'Oh!' Rivanah looked at her, pulling back her hand slightly, but Advika's left hand grasped it. It was unusually warm. They shook hands.

'Actually, I found this in my house.' She showed her the bowl and continued, 'I have no idea how it got there.'

Advika smiled, eyeing the servant, and said, 'I'd asked her to send some for you.'

'But—' Rivanah started but was cut short again.

'I love cooking. But now I can't do so myself; I only get to supervise. Is it any good?' Advika said.

'It is awesome. Just the way my mother prepares it.'

'Thank you.'

'You stay alone here?' Rivanah asked.

'Not alone. Nivan stays with me.'

'Oh, yes. That was so silly of me to ask,' Rivanah said awkwardly.

'Nivan told me about you though.'

'He did?' she asked in surprise.

'The way you made him dance at the office party. I would've loved to witness it in person.'

Rivanah desperately wanted to disappear into thin air.

'Trust me, I've known Nivan for a long time. And I'm yet to see him dance. You must be some girl to have made it possible.'

Yeah, some girl I'm! Someone with no limits to her stupidity, Rivanah thought.

'Thank you,' Advika said.

'Huh?' Rivanah wasn't prepared for it.

'Thank you for making Nivan happy. Of late, he's been quite stressed. He seldom shares his problems with me. But since that dancing incident, he has been happy. I can feel it. And I'm sure you are the reason for it.'

I am? I can't be the reason for my own happiness, how can I make someone else happy? Rivanah thought and said, 'Well, I'm sure there's a better and more legitimate reason for him to be happy.'

Advika was about to respond when Rivanah's phone rang. It was her mother.

'Excuse me,' Rivanah apologized and picked up the call.

'Mumma, what happened?'

'It's Baba here,' said Mr Bannerjee in a grave tone. Rivanah stood up and went a little away from Advika so she could speak to him privately.

'Baba, why do you sound so serious?'

'I just came back from office, so I'm a little tired. Anyway, Mini, some office work has come up in Mumbai. Mumma and I are coming over there tomorrow. What's your address? I misplaced the paper on which you wrote it down when you were here.'

Sudden work in Mumbai? Something wasn't right.

22

Rivanah took her leave from Advika soon after the phone call. She couldn't sleep properly that night. There were too many questions haunting her. Was her parents' sudden visit actually because of office work? Or were they coming to check on her? Also, what would she tell them about Danny? She'd never told them she was living with him in the first place. And now she won't have to, but should she come out clean about her relationship with him, even if it was a thing of the past now?

Upon their arrival, Mr and Mrs Bannerjee's first impression of their daughter's new place was good. But they were not in favour of the fact that she was living alone.

'What if you fall sick? There should be one roommate at least,' Mrs Bannerjee said.

'Your mother is right, Mini,' Mr Bannerjee chipped in, making himself comfortable on the sofa. He was happy there weren't any of those horrible bean bags in sight that he so greatly despised. 'I have spread the word.

Someone will join me soon,' Rivanah lied while serving her parents water.

'Which branch will you have to go to, Baba?' Rivanah asked, trying to figure out if there really was any office work.

'Wait, I have to show you something,' Mr Bannerjee said and brought out a newspaper from his bag. *Why was he evading my question?* Rivanah wondered, as he opened the newspaper's entertainment supplement. He pointed at a particular picture and gave the supplement to Rivanah. 'See.'

She took it from him with a frown. It didn't take long for her to identify Danny in the photograph. He was with three girls and two boys. The photograph was part of a feature whose headline read 'Newbies in Bollywood'. She took half a minute to go through the article. It was the first unofficial announcement of the movie Danny was doing. *Finally he has made it*, she thought. Just when she was out of his life.

'Don't tell me, Baba, you guys came to Mumbai for this?' Rivanah said.

'Of course not. But it's good to know that Danny's movie will be coming out soon,' Mr Bannerjee said.

Rivanah glanced at her mother who beamed at her as if she was happy that her daughter would now be allowed to marry the guy of her choice.

'It doesn't matter,' Rivanah said. While reading the article, she had decided it was useless to keep them in the dark.

'What do you mean?' Mrs Bannerjee's smile disappeared at once.

'We broke up.'

Mr Bannerjee threw an incredulous look at his wife and said the expected; 'I told you!'

Rivanah sat back on the sofa trying to shut her mind because she knew most of what was going to be said. And when it was over, Rivanah said, 'This is what you guys wanted anyway. Why dissect it more?'

Both Mr and Mrs Bannerjee understood their daughter had a point. Mr Bannerjee quietly went inside to change while Mrs Bannerjee came close to her daughter and asked, 'One last question, Mini.'

'What?'

'Why did you two break up?'

Rivanah rolled her eyes and said, 'That's because we stopped loving each other.' She carried their luggage to the guest bedroom while her mother mumbled under her breath, 'Stopped loving each other? How ridiculous!'

When Rivanah came out of the bedroom, she saw her parents gaping at the sketch stand.

'What happened?'

'Who sketched this?' Mr Bannerjee asked. He sounded as grave as he did on the phone when he had informed her about his Mumbai trip.

'Someone who used to stay here before me.'

'What?' Mr Bannerjee said in shock.

'That's what the landlord told me. But why do you look so unconvinced? Have you seen the sketch somewhere?'

Before Mr Bannerjee could speak, his wife spoke up, 'How will we see the sketch before? You sketched it in Kolkata also, so your baba must have thought—'

'What? I sketched this in Kolkata? When?' Rivanah said, looking at her parents. She noticed her father shooting an angry glance at her mother as if she had crossed a line, and then he said, 'Not exactly this, but you used to sketch facial portraits during your schooldays.'

There was an awkward silence in the room for some time.

'Is this our room?' Mr Bannerjee asked.

'No. This is mine. Yours is the other one. I have kept the luggage inside.'

'Good. And you shouldn't keep other people's stuff with you. It's not good manners,' Mr Bannerjee said, pointing to the sketch one last time, and then went away.

'Your baba is right.' Mrs Bannerjee came to her daughter and grasped her hand. 'One can't trust anyone or anything.'

'What are you talking about, Mumma? It's just a sketch stand for God's sake. Anyway, I'm going to take a bath now and then I have to rush to office. Everything is in the kitchen, Mumma. By the way, when do you have to go to office, Baba?' Rivanah wanted an answer.

'What's the hurry?' Mr Bannerjee said, unlocking his suitcase and averting his eyes.

'Baba, look at me,' Rivanah said. 'There's no office work, right?'

Mr Bannerjee looked down at the suitcase making the answer evident.

'Can't we come to just see you, Mini?' Mrs Bannerjee joined them in the bedroom.

'Of course, Mumma, you can. Any time. But what's the reason to lie?'

'We thought you may ask us to delay the visit if we were coming only to see you,' Mrs Bannerjee said.

'Okay, whatever. You guys take rest now,' she said and went to take a bath.

Rivanah reached her office and immediately messaged the Stranger: *Is the question you wanted me to ask myself and my parents' Mumbai visit connected?*

The Stranger's response made Rivanah's heart skip a beat: *Very much.*

Rivanah couldn't believe the fact that her own parents were probably part of something sinister. Did they know who the Stranger was? Her fingers trembled as she typed a message back: *How are the two connected?*

I shall only provide you with the dots. You'll have to draw the line yourself, Mini.

Damn! She was frustrated about the whole thing. And scared too, knowing her parents were hiding something on which perhaps two of the biggest questions in her life depended: one; what connected her to Hiya Chowdhury, and two, who the hell was this Stranger? A direct confrontation with her parents on this, she now knew, wouldn't fetch the kind of results she wanted. Rivanah kept pondering over this all day. In between, she checked Danny's Facebook profile. As expected, the Add as a Friend button showed up. She had been ousted from there too. *If that's what you want, Danny,* she thought and logged out.

Rivanah received a call from Sadhu Ram inquiring if anything untoward had happened after they had caught Argho at Bungalow 9. Rivanah informed him she would like to take the complaint back, realizing the Stranger puzzle wasn't going to end with the help of police. In fact, it would only become more complicated. She would have to solve it on her own. *If at all it is solvable,* she thought.

In the evening, when Rivanah reached her place, she ran into Nivan taking a stroll with Xeno in the society premises.

'You came early?' Rivanah said, kneeling down to pat Xeno on the head.

'I was in Bangalore for a meeting. Came a few hours back. How is it going?'

'All good.'

'I'm sure. I heard your parents are here,' she heard Nivan say.

'Oh yes, they are.'

'Nice. See you around,' he said and pulled Xeno away. He had taken a couple of steps when Rivanah rushed to him.

'Do you, by any chance, remember who your last tenant was?' Rivanah asked.

'Well, it was a guy.'

'Okay.' Rivanah's hair on her nape rose. *Was it the Stranger?*

'What did he look like?' Rivanah asked, anxious.

'Don't mind me asking, but what's up? Is there any problem?'

Rivanah immediately realized her mistake. 'I'm sorry I'm being rude,' she said and tried to act all normal. 'My father saw the sketch stand and wanted me to return it to the person who left it there since he doesn't like to use other people's things.'

'To be honest, it has been some time the guy lived here. And I was in the US at that time. I don't really remember him clearly. But I think if he left the sketch stand here, it must mean it wasn't important to him or else he would have come back.'

Makes sense, Rivanah thought.

'If you want I can get it removed.'

'It's okay. It's a sketch stand, after all. Not a time bomb.' Rivanah managed a smile. Nivan too smiled back. He finally walked away with Xeno while Rivanah entered the building. By the time she reached the sixteenth floor, she had an idea—as the Stranger had said— to join the dots.

Rivanah remained quiet all through dinner. She told her parents she had had a long day in office and would retire early. She waited for her parents to sleep, after which she tiptoed into their room. She looked around and soon found her father's phone on the bedside table. It was an old phone without any password protection. She quickly unlocked it and went to Contacts and scrolled down. Rivanah sighed in relief, seeing what she was hoping for: Manick Dutta's phone number. She typed a message to him: *It was nice to meet you the other day. Hope you are doing fine.*

Rivanah sent it, praying that Mr Dutta was awake. It was only 10.45 p.m., after all. Not everyone slept early like her parents. Putting the phone on mute, she waited impatiently for a response. Her father turned around in his sleep. Rivanah froze. She had an excuse ready: if any of the two woke up, she would tell them she had come to look for a hairclip. But neither woke up.

Two minutes later, a message came in from Mr Dutta: *The pleasure is mine. It was indeed nice to meet you and family the other day. I hope Rivanah is all right.*

She is fine. Thank you. Rivanah messaged back, now certain that the visit to Mr Dutta's house wasn't a dream as she was made to believe by her parents. *But why? What happened at Mr Manick Dutta's place which had to be kept a secret from me by my own parents?* Rivanah deleted all the messages and put the phone back on the side table.

23

'Is there anything that you are hiding from us, Mini?' Mr Bannerjee asked.

It was next morning. The three were at the dining table having breakfast. Mr Bannerjee was reading the *Economic Times* while Mrs Bannerjee was leafing through the entertainment section. She glanced at her husband and then at her daughter, anticipating a response from the latter.

The word 'hiding' made Rivanah look up for the first time since she had joined her parents for breakfast. She couldn't sleep after reading Mr Dutta's message. What was it her parents were hiding from her? Why would her own parents hide anything from her in the first place? And now her father was asking her what *she* was hiding?

'Nothing, why?' she said.

'You seem lost. Didn't you sleep well?'

'Office pressure,' she said and noticed her parents exchanging looks. *This exchange of looks*, Rivanah surmised, *has happened too many times since they came here.*

'Don't let your health get affected, shona,' Mrs Bannerjee said. They resumed eating in silence.

'I'll get ready for office.' Rivanah went to her room after breakfast, while Mrs Bannerjee cleared the table and took the leftovers back to the kitchen. Just then, Mr Bannerjee heard two screams—one came from the bedroom and the other from the kitchen. Mr Bannerjee didn't know where to go. He scampered to the kitchen and realized his wife was standing with her hands on her hips while the washbasin tap was flowing with full gusto.

'Why don't you close the tap? You are wasting water.'

'It won't close.'

Mr Bannerjee came to inspect the tap and splashed water all over him in the process. He understood the knot in the tap had become loose.

'Why did you open it so hard?' he asked, irritated. 'We have to bring a plumber for this.'

Rivanah dashed into the kitchen, asking, 'Where did you put the sketch, Mumma? Why isn't it there on the sketch stand?'

'I just kept it—'

'And what's this?' Rivanah asked, gaping at the water gushing out of the tap. Her father had tied a piece of cloth over the tap, controlling the force of the water somewhat.

'Call a plumber, Mini,' Mr Bannerjee said.

'I have no idea where from. Wait, let me ask Nivan.'

'Who is Nivan?' Mrs Bannerjee was instantly curious.

'My landlord,' Rivanah said and left the kitchen.

Nivan answered the doorbell. He was in a tee and shorts, coffee mug in hand.

'Hey,' he said.

'Hi,' she replied, while trying hard not to register the boyish charm he exuded. She failed miserably.

'Do you know a plumber around here? The kitchen tap has gone bonkers.'

'Oh.' Nivan kept the coffee mug on the wooden shoe rack and came out of the flat.

'Let me check.'

'A plumber would do actually,' Rivanah said, feeling embarrassed about her senior trying a role shift.

'It's okay.'

Rivanah reluctantly led him inside the flat and into the kitchen where her parents were still fidgeting with the tap. Rivanah made a quick introduction as Nivan went towards the kitchen window, opened it completely and stretched his hand out.

'Its main knob is outside,' he said and the water stopped immediately. Nivan drew his hand in and said, 'I shall send the plumber in some time.'

'Thank you so much, Mr Nivan . . .' Mr Bannerjee was fetching for a surname and Rivanah knew exactly why.

'Mallick. Nivan Mallick.'

'It is nice to meet you, Mr Mallick.'

'Same here, sir,' Nivan said.

'Thanks for taking such good care of my daughter. She told me everything,' he said with a smile. Though it was a lie—*she told me everything*— Rivanah knew where the discussion was heading and wanted to stop her father right there but couldn't.

'Your daughter deserves every bit of it.'

'Why don't you join us for dinner tonight if it's not much of a problem?'

There! She knew it.

'Baba, he is a busy man.' Rivanah had to barge in now.

'Why, don't busy people have dinner?' he said and laughed, aptly joined by his wife.

'I would love to. I love Bong food.' Nivan said.

'Khoob bhalo! Then at 9 tonight?'

'Sure.'

Rivanah escorted Nivan to the main door and shut it after him. She was about to rush to the kitchen but she noticed her parents were already in the drawing room.

'Very nice boy,' Mr Bannerjee said.

'Shotti!' Mrs Bannerjee confirmed her husband's sentiments.

'He is my senior in office, Baba.'

'Senior? What's his designation?'

'VP, sales.'

'VP? This is even better. At such a young age. He must be what, 28–29? Max 30. A real achiever indeed. He must have good genes.'

Rivanah knew arguing would be a waste of time. She changed the topic. 'Where's the sketch, Mumma?'

'I have kept it inside the wardrobe.

'Why? Was it biting you?'

'Why keep someone else's sketch in the open?'

'Uff, tumi je ki koro na!' Rivanah walked off.

In the office, Rivanah thought the best way to avoid the impending dinner disaster would be to somehow request Nivan not to come for dinner. She didn't have his phone number yet. And going to his cabin for such a lame thing would be too much. She went through her mails to check if any of them had Nivan's official mail ID. She found it in one of the group emails. She immediately wrote to him. *May I have your mobile number?*

A minute later, Nivan replied with his phone number. Rivanah saved it on her phone and checked if he was available on WhatsApp. He was. She typed carefully: *Sorry to disturb you like this, but I hope my parents didn't offend you in any way.*

His reply came soon enough: *Offended? Not at all. Looking forward to some delicious Bong food tonight.*

And Rivanah knew an acute embarrassment was only hours away.

Mrs Bannerjee surprised Rivanah with the number of food items she had prepared for dinner.

'Mumma, he is coming alone, not with the whole colony. Why have you prepared so much food?'

'I know, but what will he think of us if we don't give him options?'

The acute embarrassment was confirmed as far as Rivanah was concerned. Not because she had any problem with so many food items, but because she knew what the intention behind impressing Nivan was.

The doorbell rang shortly after nine. Mr Bannerjee welcomed Nivan. The dinner didn't go as badly as Rivanah had imagined. Nivan loved everything that was served to him. Mr Bannerjee found the perfect pal in Nivan to discuss his latest obsession: politics. Seeing Nivan talk with her father, she remembered how Danny too had once come for dinner only to be cold-shouldered by her father. *How lifesaving it would be if one already knew whether a relationship would go the distance or not, before commencing it. We can always change the road we take but we can't undo the steps we took.*

It was around 10.30 when Nivan finally left. Rivanah let out a sigh of relief as she joined her parents on the couch in the drawing room.

'Mini,' Mr Bannerjee said and continued once Rivanah looked up at him, 'I think Nivan is a good guy.'

'Hmm.' Rivanah said.

'I think we should meet his parents too.'

'Huh?'

'He is young, highly qualified, seems very decent, knowledgeable, well settled, and he is not married.'

Rivanah was in an instant dilemma: whether to feel happy about all this or to rue over the fact that her father actually made such enquiries.

'Baba, don't tell me you asked him if he was married.'

'I did when you went to the kitchen to fetch more water for him.'

'But why?'

'What why? It is pretty evident what your choice of guys is like. I think you should focus on your job and let us select your life partner. And don't worry, we won't give you any reason to cry about this.'

'I know that, Baba, but I don't even know Nivan.'

'You always told us you knew Ekansh and Danny. What was the result? Marriage is about taking as much time as possible to know the person. You youngsters end up knowing everyone so quickly that you get bored and itch to move on to someone else.'

'This is not what happened with Ekansh or Danny.'

'You told us what happened between Ekansh and you, but what happened with Danny?' Mrs Bannerjee was curious.

Rivanah threw a helpless look at her mother and then said, 'Nothing. I'm feeling tired. Goodnight.' As she hit the bed, her father's words echoed in her mind: *and he is not married*. Why did that sound so appealing? In the Stranger's words: was she yet again seeking a bigger and deeper hurt in Nivan in order to get over the one given by Danny? It had been some time since the Stranger had contacted her. And with the house-hunting and shifting and her parents' arrival, she didn't get the time to contact him more than once. She knew now was the time.

You there? she messaged on one of the stored numbers.

You bet, was the immediate response.

A smile lit up her face. *How are you?*

I'm good, Mini. Thank you for asking. How are you?

I'm . . . I don't know. Tell me, you wanted to kill me some time back, and now you don't contact me at all. Why are you so unpredictable?

I'm unpredictable because you know nothing about me, but in your mind you have heaps of presumptions about me.

Why don't you clear those presumptions then?

I will when I'm in the mood, Mini.

You never will, I know.

That too is a presumption.

Haha. Okay, what if I say I know you are aware of the fact that I live right next to Nivan's flat. Would you call it a presumption?

No. I will call it duty. My duty is to know whatever you are up to.

I knew that. What if I tell you I've been thinking about Nivan? Do you think I'm doing so because I'm somewhere seeking a bigger and deeper hurt?

Perhaps.

What should I do then?

Be wary of Nivan. He is hiding something.

For the first time during the chat, Rivanah's expression changed into a deep frown. *What is it?*

It is something that may bring you and me closer. Goodnight, Mini.
Rivanah messaged back couple of times but there
was no response. *What could Nivan possibly be hiding that
may bring the Stranger closer to me?* Rivanah wondered and
replayed the entire evening in her mind from the time
he came in. She stopped at a particular moment when
he had asked her if the sketch stand had to be removed.
Rivanah had said no, after which he had asked if she
had found anything else that belonged to the previous
tenant. She had said no then, but the truth was that she
had not checked the flat thoroughly.

Rivanah got up with a start, closed her room's door
lest her parents noticed, and switched on the light. She
checked the wardrobe, behind it, under the bed, below
the mattress. While lifting the mattress, she noticed the
bed had boxes for storage. Three out of the four boxes
were empty. In the fourth box, she found a stack of
books. They were some old Harold Robbins and Irving
Wallace books. She was about to put them back in the
box when she noticed something white peeping out of
one of the books. She opened the particular novel and her
jaw dropped immediately. It was a white piece of cloth
with a message embroidered in black thread. She quickly
opened the other books and all of them had a similar
white cloth on which some message was embroidered in
black. The sight made her stomach churn.

24

The radium hands of the clock in Rivanah's bedroom showed it was 3.15 a.m. As she tossed and turned in bed, Rivanah felt she couldn't move her hands properly. She got up and tried to move one hand but realized it was tied to the other.

'Fuck!' she gasped.

A sound made her look towards the window. She saw a man's silhouette, clear against the moonlight by the room's window. He had a shiny object in his hand.

'Hello, Mini,' the man said.

She knew who it was. She had asked him on the skywalk if he wanted to kill her. The sight of the shiny, pointy object told her he did. She tried to jump out of the bed and fell on the floor. Her feet were free but her hands were tied. She was about to scream when she heard the Stranger say, 'If you call your parents, I'll kill you in two seconds, but if you keep quiet and cooperate I shall tell you who I am.'

Rivanah, still on the floor, was already breathing hard. Her lower lip quivered. And her silence told the

Stranger what her decision was. With each step he took towards her, her heartbeat quickened. He bent down and picked her up in his arms, as if she were a feather. His strength aroused her and eclipsed her fear even. The mask covering his face revealed only his eyes, lips and the tip of his nose. She knew she had seen those eyes before.

He took her to the drawing room, never breaking eye contact.

The Stranger placed her close to the glass wall. Before her feet could find the floor, he pursed her lips with his. In a second, his tongue barged into her mouth. The hunger with which he was exploring her mouth broke the slumber created by fear in her, and every inch of her body awoke to an overtly sexual dawn. She wanted to see who this Stranger was but her hands were still tied together. He broke off the kiss and, looking straight into her eyes, tore open her nightdress. The buttons flew open, and he doffed the shirt as she raised her hands above her head. Rivanah rarely wore a bra at night, and her breasts were now out in the open. Her instinct was to cover them with her hands but they were pinned above her head with such power that she didn't even try. The Stranger squeezed her breasts with his free hand and whispered in her ears, 'I'm going to untie you now. I hope you know what you have to do.' With a deadly twinkle in his eyes, he slowly pulled a string and her hands came free. She put her arms around him immediately and pulled him closer to cover her breasts with his chest. Holding him around his neck with one hand, her other hand slithered downwards till it reached his groin. As she massaged his erect penis over his jeans, she pulled his face closer to hers and this time explored his mouth herself with a renewed hunger. The Stranger grasped her hand over his groin. He made her unzip his jeans, and then tug it down, along with his underwear, till his knees. She could feel the tip of his erect penis poking her lower abdomen over her shorts as the two smooched harder. The Stranger scratched her thighs and reached for the elastic of her shorts. Slowly, he rolled both her shorts and panties down together. Grabbing her bare butt with his strong hands, he lifted her till both her legs were resting on his arm. Next, he brought her down so that she could hold his penis and guide it inside her. She obliged and let out a loud moan as he entered her. She heard some noise in her parent's bedroom. *What if my mother comes out in the drawing room right now? What will I tell her?* The forbidden nature of her act made Rivanah even more excited. As the Stranger kept moving his pelvis against hers with vigour, Rivanah kept glancing at her parents' door, hoping nobody came out, while her heart wanted the Stranger to keep going. The way he was looking at her told her he knew what was on her mind . . .

After this, you'll have to remove the mask. You'll have to tell me who you are. I promise I won't tell anyone anything. Not even my parents or the police. I have paid enough price to deserve your identity now, Stranger. Even if you want to kill me after this, do it. I wouldn't mind, but here's one last wish: I want to die in your arms, Stranger. I want to die in your arms, looking deep into your eyes as you lead me to a crushing climax where life and death merge to become eternity . . .

'Mini?' Mrs Bannerjee called out from her room. By the time she came into Rivanah's bedroom inquiring who she was talking to at such an odd hour, Rivanah was sound asleep—or faking it, to be more precise. Mrs Bannerjee came to her, caressed her forehead and then returned to her room. Once Rivanah was sure her mother had gone, she opened her eyes. Her heart was racing. She couldn't believe she had spoken the words out loud, with her parents in the very next room. She removed her hand from between her legs, tugged her panties up and sat up. Her fantasy had ended abruptly. She felt a little empty, but she didn't want to do it again.

Rivanah went into the washroom and shut the door. Switching on the lights, Rivanah stared at her reflection in the mirror. She saw someone who had no clue what was happening in her life. After she had found the pieces of white cloth inside the books, Rivanah had been shell-shocked for some time. They had the same messages that she had received from the Stranger in the beginning. Was it the Stranger who had stayed in this flat before her? Her parents were surely hiding something. The Stranger wouldn't tell her anything directly, so where did that leave her? Whom could she talk to? She felt a stifling restlessness which wouldn't let her sleep or even be at peace. She wanted a distraction. The Stranger had come into her life once in a while, and it ended in a raunchy fantasy. But the questions still remained: whom could she talk to about the pieces of cloth? And why would the Stranger say Nivan was hiding something?

The next morning, her mother complained that Rivanah hadn't taken a day off work to spend time with her parents, like she had done the last time they had come to Mumbai.

'But, Mumma, I don't have many leaves. And I've just joined this company,' she said but promised herself to take her parents out for dinner at least.

At work, she kept thinking of how she could find out more about the pieces of cloth in the bed box. She was surprised when Nivan messaged her asking her to come to his cabin whenever she was free. Rivanah went to him immediately.

'Good morning, Rivanah,' he said.

'Hello, Nivan.'

'Sorry to have disturbed you during work hours.'

'Not a problem,' she said and wondered if she should tell him about the pieces of cloth.

'You look like you have something to share?' Nivan said.

'Actually, I stumbled upon some white pieces of cloth in my bed box.'

'White cloth?' Nivan looked interested.

'Pieces of cloth with messages embroidered on them.'

'That's weird.'

Nivan clearly had no idea how those could have ended up in the bed box. Rivanah decided to drop the matter and take it up on her own later.

'Anyway, you called me. Anything important?' she said.

'Yes. I looked for the agreement which I had with the previous resident of the flat.'

You are a saviour, Nivan, Rivanah thought. 'Thank you so much.'

Nivan picked up a document and gave it to Rivanah, saying, 'Never mind. This is the agreement. The tenant's name is Ekansh Tripathi.'

Rivanah looked down at the name on the document. For a moment, her mind went blank. She slowly lifted her face, still unable to think properly.

'Your expression tells me you know the person.'

'Umm . . .' She felt her throat had dried up by then. 'Not really,' she lied.

'Okay. He has a phone number if you can read it in the agreement. If you want you call him up and talk about the sketch stand.'

There was no response from Rivanah.

'Hello? Everything okay?' Nivan said, leaning forward.

'Yeah,' Rivanah nodded, looking stumped. 'Yeah, right. I'll call him.'

'Great.'

She took her leave. Back in her cubicle, Rivanah had only one question on her mind: *when* would Ekansh

Tripathi leave her life? She had deleted his number but it was still etched in her mind. She matched it with the one in the agreement—they were the same. She dialled, but before it could connect, Rivanah cut the call. She still wasn't sure if she should give Ekansh another excuse to enter her life. Especially since what happened the last time they met had altered her life drastically. She put these thoughts away and dialled again. The call was answered on the third ring.

'Hi, Rivanah. What's up?' he said in a formal tone.

That voice . . . that 'Hi Rivanah' . . . that 'what's up' . . . they were like the evil chant of a witch to crack open her box of memories, which had nothing but pain and suffering in the form of beautiful snapshots of the past.

'Did you ever live in the Residency Enclave, B wing, flat no. 1604?'

'What?'

'Please answer me.'

There was a pause.

'I think so.'

'Did you or did you not?'

'I did. For some time when I . . .' He stopped midway.

You were cheating on me. Rivanah completed his sentence in her mind.

'But Tista once told me you lived in Navi Mumbai.'

'That was after this. Why are you asking?'

Rivanah quickly checked the date on the agreement. The stay in the Residency Enclave was indeed dated well before she had moved in with Tista.

'Hello? You there, Rivanah?' Ekansh said.

'Please don't ever take my name,' she said and asked, 'Did you keep a sketch stand in the flat?'

'A sketch stand? I never used to sketch, you did. Why are you asking me all this? And what about Danny? Is everything okay? Look, I'm really sorry for my behaviour that day.'

The mention of Danny's name pushed her to remember how she had kissed Ekansh and sent the picture of it to Danny. Disgust clouded her.

'Yeah. All is fine. Bye.' She cut the line. Ekansh called back. Rivanah ignored the call, and later blocked the number. *Whom should I trust? Ekansh? The guy who has already given me the biggest reason in the past not to trust him?* A dreaded thought occurred to her at that moment: what if Ekansh was the Stranger? A mild headache hit her and she started massaging her forehead.

'Hey, what happened? You okay?' Smita enquired.

'Nothing,' Rivanah muttered. She somehow managed to get back to work.

In the evening, Rivanah left office later than usual. She called her parents and asked them to come over to Red Box in Andheri itself. She met them downstairs, and together they went up to the restaurant. Though she maintained a smile all through the dinner, there was too much on her mind for her to enjoy. They were done in two hours and took an autorickshaw home. As they were about to walk into the elevator, they bumped into Nivan. Greetings were exchanged. But Rivanah sensed something wasn't right about him. When she reached the sixteenth floor, she received a message from Nivan: *Come downstairs, please.*

With a slight frown, Rivanah told her parents she would join them in few minutes and took the elevator down. The moment she stepped out of the elevator, she noticed Nivan's BMW right outside the building. He was behind the wheel. She walked up to him, but before she could enquire, he said, 'Get inside.'

Rivanah got in and asked, 'What happened?'

Nivan pointed to something on the dashboard as he shifted the gear. Rivanah noticed there were two Post-it notes stuck on it.

The first one read: *I lied to you.*

The one right beside it read: *I'd kept the pieces of cloth in the books inside the bed box.*

They had driven out of the Residency Enclave by then.

25

Reading the two Post-it notes, Rivanah got goosebumps all over her body. She sat stiff as Nivan drove the car rather unsteadily. Perhaps he too was unnerved by something. For the first few minutes, Rivanah kept quiet, hoping Nivan would clarify what he meant when he said he kept the pieces of cloth inside the bed. Was he the Stranger? It sounded absurd.

'Could you please—' she began, but Nivan grabbed her hand. She stopped. He moved his hand from the gear and quickly stuck another Post-it on the dashboard. Rivanah looked down to realize he had a bunch of those notes beside the gear. The note said: *Sshhh.*

Nivan stuck another one.

I have checked myself and the car. Are you sure you aren't bugged? Just nod if you aren't. Or else, check.

Rivanah remembered how her dress had been once bugged by the Stranger. She tapped the edges of her shirt, the sleeves, the shoulder, the buttons, the trouser and finally her footwear. Nothing seemed suspicious. She nodded to Nivan. He put another note on the dashboard:

Don't talk till I stop the car.

Nivan drove to the western express highway and then, paying the toll, entered the 7-km-long Worli Sea Link. At night, the city skyline on both sides of the Sea Link made Mumbai look like a teenager's first love: too good to be real.

The car slowly came to a halt in the middle of the Sea Link. They both stepped out. Nivan went in front of the car and opened the bonnet. Rivanah joined him.

'Are you being pursued by someone?' Nivan asked, without looking at her. She nodded hesitantly.

'Same here,' he muttered.

'What do you mean?' Rivanah said, as a breeze ruffled her hair. She tucked her hair behind her ears. Nivan looked around and then, staring at the car's engine in front of him, said, 'Two years ago, it started with a rather harmless note saying: *Be ready, Nivan.*'

The scene inside the Meru cab when she arrived in Mumbai for the first time flashed in her mind: *Be ready, Mini.*

'Then one message after another started coming in. Pieces of white cloth in which the messages were embroidered in black thread.'

Nothing made sense to Rivanah.

'I went to the police as well but it didn't help. The person isn't just a stalker. He made me do weird things like . . .'

'Like?' Rivanah's throat was dry.

'Like . . .' Nivan glanced at Rivanah and said, 'Make sure you were employed in our company.'

While I was left with no other option but to seek your company out, Rivanah thought and said aloud, 'Do you mean you always knew who I was?'

'You were just a name to me, and one of the tasks I was given by this . . .'

'Stranger.' Rivanah completed his sentence for him. Nivan nodded.

'And you had to do it?' she asked.

Nivan nodded again. Just like she *had to* do what the Stranger wanted.

'So I had kept the cloth pieces inside the bed box. Those were given to me. Did you get them as well?'

'Yes. I did,' Rivanah said, matching Nivan's soft tone. 'But didn't you try to find out who the Stranger is or why he is pursuing you?'

'I tried my best but couldn't. I don't even try to trace him any more. But I am sure my moves are under observation,' he said in a resigned tone.

Hence the Post-it notes, Rivanah thought and said, 'Are you still in touch with the Stranger?'

'I was never in touch with him. It was he who never left me.'

They fell silent.

'I sensed it the day you came to my cabin and told me about the pieces of cloth. And tonight, I only wanted to make sure if it was what I thought it was. That you too are a victim of this mysterious frenemy, who coincidentally we both refer to as the Stranger,' Nivan said as he closed the bonnet.

'Let's go back. Please don't mention this conversation to the Stranger, in case you are in touch with him.'

Rivanah nodded. As they got back inside the car, Rivanah was tempted to ask Nivan if he had a personal secret because of which the Stranger was in his life— just like Hiya was her secret which the Stranger wanted her to pursue. And whether his and her secrets have a link. Rivanah took one of the Post-it notes. Nivan's eyes followed Rivanah as she opened the glovebox. She found a pen and immediately scribbled on the slip. She showed it to Nivan.

Is the Stranger making you seek some secret?

She sensed a tinge of discomfort on Nivan's face as he stepped on the accelerator and murmured, 'I can't tell you.'

Which means there is one, Rivanah concluded. She checked her phone which she had left inside the car. There were five missed calls from her father's number. She didn't call back.

When Rivanah returned to her flat, her parents kept hounding her, enquiring where she had disappeared. They stopped bothering her when she told them she was with Nivan. It seemed to make them happy. But Rivanah wasn't happy. After what Nivan had told her, she only had one priority now: to find out about Hiya Chowdhury. That's the link to the Stranger. And why would he involve Nivan in the scheme of things? So many times she was on the verge of inquiring about Hiya—and the sketch—to her parents, but she didn't. If her parents were to tell her something, they would have done so by now. She would have to find out in a different way.

Retiring to her room, Rivanah put the sketch back on the sketch stand and kept staring at it. Was the sketch the sole clue in the entire puzzle? On a hunch, she stood up, removed the sketch and stared at the blank page on the stand. She took a deep breath and walked to her dressing table. She brought her eye pencil and stood in front of the sketch stand once again. Letting her instinct take over, she started sketching. When she was done, Rivanah's sketch quite resembled the one that had been on the stand earlier. It scared her, but she knew she was right. The sketch was a clue. She took a good picture of the sketch and uploaded it on Facebook with a question: *Whom does she resemble?*

She kept refreshing the page but there came no likes or comments. Frustrated, she slumped on her bed again. It was around 4.30 a.m. when her eyes opened suddenly. She checked her phone. There was one comment on the picture. She immediately tapped on the notification. Someone by the name of Binay Das had liked the picture and left a comment: *Isn't that our college-mate Hiya?* And Rivanah knew she was closer to unveiling the mystery than she had ever been. She left a message for Binay asking him to call her on her number the moment he saw the message.

She couldn't get much sleep that night. It was 8 a.m. when her phone rang.

'Hi, this is Binay here. How are you doing, Rivanah? It has been so long. Where are you?'

She remembered Binay from college as someone who would take fifty words to say what could be said in five.

'Binay, don't get me wrong, but I need to know something urgently. We will talk properly later.'

'Sure. What happened?'

'You commented on the picture I put up.'

'That's Hiya Chowdhury, right?'

'What do you know about her?'

'About Hiya? The usual, that she was our batch topper and the one who committed suicide.'

'That's it?'

'And you two were fierce competitors.'

Just the kind of information I am looking for. 'Anything else?' she said.

'Ummm. Can't think of anything else right now. Why do you need to know about Hiya, all of a sudden?'

'Just like that.'

'Okay. Where are you, by the way?'

'Mumbai.'

'Great, I'm in Pune. I can come down this weekend if you—'

'I'm really busy this weekend, Binay. I'll call when I'm free. You take care. Bye.' She quickly cut the line and blocked the number. She had no room in her life for guys who mistook her friendliness for availability.

Rivanah now had two clues: she had sketched Hiya's face again and again, and the two had been fierce competitors in college. The fact that her father told her she used to sketch in school could well be a lie. But why would this sketch and stand be in this flat? And a sketch stand was in the Krishna Towers flat as well. Something told her she was there and yet not there.

'Didn't you sleep properly?' her mother asked walking into her room.

'Yes, I did. Let me go for a bath, Mumma. Need to go to office early today.'

Mrs Bannerjee sensed something was not all right.

'You better be back early today,' Mrs Bannerjee said, as her daughter entered the bathroom. 'Your baba and I are leaving tonight, remember?'

The latching of the bathroom door was the only response.

At work, Rivanah wrote down the supposed dots on a piece of paper. Telling Nivan about it verbally could be risky. Writing it down was the best option—like they had done in the car the other night.

Parents are hiding something . . . Hiya Chowdhury's sketch in my flat . . . she's my college-mate who hanged herself . . . I was able to sketch her face even though I supposedly stopped sketching long back . . . Hiya was my competition in college, but I don't remember anything about her . . . in fact, recently I forgot all about her, though I had gone to unearth the missing link in Kolkata . . . father's colleague—Mr Dutta—seems a shady character . . . Argho Chowdhury is Hiya's cousin, but I doubt he is involved in this. These are the dots which, I'm sure, lead somewhere. What do I do? Please suggest.

Rivanah reread it and, once convinced she had written whatever she had in mind, went to Nivan's cabin. A look at her and Nivan knew it wasn't an official visit. She quietly passed the note to him. He read the note and seemed pensive for some time. Finally he wrote back on the paper:

Your past is in Kolkata. Don't you think going there will take us closer to the mystery?

Rivanah read the note and then looked up at Nivan.

26

'You can ask Nivan to stay with us. Why else have we built so many rooms in our house? Only for guests to come and stay,' said Mr Bannerjee the moment Rivanah told them she and Nivan would be returning with them to Kolkata on account of some office work.

'Thanks for this, Nivan. I really needed someone to—' Rivanah had told Nivan when he said he would accompany her to Kolkata. He had cut her short and said, 'There's nothing to thank me for. You forget that we both are victims. And my itch to know who this Stranger is just as strong as yours. He made me manipulate your selection in the company. I really want to know how you and I are related. If at all, that is.'

Rivanah could identify with Nivan's sentiments. The fact that they were sailing in the same boat gave her hope. Of late, she had been missing Danny. Or was she missing someone's safety net around her? Was it again the Cinderella Syndrome popping up like the psychiatrist had once told her? It was worse that she couldn't talk to the Stranger. It wasn't the time to engage in any philosophical prattle with him. It was time to end whatever shit he had been involving her in.

The Bannerjee family met Nivan after the security check in the airport. Mr Bannerjee was extra talkative to him. Rivanah had requested her family not to ask Nivan to stay at their place because it looked thoroughly unprofessional. Mrs Bannerjee, on the other hand, whispered to her daughter, 'Mini, is something going on between you two?'

'No, Mumma,' Rivanah said and excused herself to go and fetch a Coke. Anything to avoid her parents. This was something she had expected to happen. Nivan and the Bannerjee family split up and went to their assigned seats after boarding. Rivanah's parents fell asleep soon after take-off, while Rivanah watched darkness fall outside the window. In a matter of just two years, she was done with two guys—Ekansh and Danny—and now, suddenly, the rest of her life looked like those white balls of cloud—empty. She felt an urge to cry but checked herself. She went to the lavatory and looked at herself in the small mirror and wondered if she hadn't really changed. Life had only dug out another Rivanah from within her. *Not Life*, she corrected herself, *there was another name for it—the Stranger.* Since she had come to Mumbai, her life had been all about him. She hoped this visit to Kolkata would end the mystery. Rivanah was walking back to her seat when she heard her name. She turned around and saw Nivan sitting in the last row. The entire row was empty. Rivanah gladly joined him.

'Did the Stranger get in touch?' he asked.

'Not after last time.'

'I thought so. It only means we are following what he wants us to follow.'

'I agree.'

'I was wondering if you know anyone in Kolkata who would be able to give us any information about Hiya Chowdhury.'

Rivanah thought for a minute and said, 'Ishita, a friend of mine. She was the one who told me I'd forgotten about Hiya suddenly.'

'Hmm, okay. This forgetting part confused me, actually. How can a person forget something all of a sudden, unless it is some sort of amnesia?'

'I know. But the weirdest thing is, although I'd forgotten everything about Hiya, I remembered the Stranger.'

Nivan's eyes remained on Rivanah for some time as if he was trying to figure out what the reason could be.

'Anyway, we should meet your friend first,' he said.

'Sure.'

Rivanah soon joined her parents and found them still asleep. She didn't wake them up lest they probed her more about Nivan.

The flight landed on time. Nivan headed to ITC Sonar Bangla, while Rivanah and her parents took a cab home. She couldn't wait to call Ishita. Once home, Rivanah went straight to the terrace and called her.

'Hey babe, what's up?'

Rivanah could hear loud music. 'Go to a quieter place.'

'Give me a second.'

As Rivanah held on, Ishita spoke a few seconds later.

'Better?'

'Much better. I'm in Kolkata.'

'Cool. Let's catch up tomorrow then?'

'Yes. Can we catch up in the morning itself?'

'I have to go to work, my dear.'

'It's urgent.'

Ishita thought for a second and said, 'Can you come down to sector 5?'

'I can come anywhere.'

'Great. There's a CCD near my office. Let's meet there. 10?'

'Absolutely.'

'All fine?'

'Almost fine. Let's talk tomorrow.'

Rivanah then dialled Nivan's number but had to end the call abruptly since she heard someone say two words.

'Hello, Mini.'

Rivanah looked towards the water tank which was not very well lit. She was sure the voice had come from there. Fear written all over her face, Rivanah tried to locate the obvious source of the voice.

'How come you are here?' she blurted.

'I go wherever you go, Mini,' the Stranger said. He was merely a voice coming out from somewhere near the water tank. In a flash, Rivanah leapt towards the switchboard and pressed the switch for the light above the water tank. Nothing happened—except, a lightbulb rolled towards her.

'Try, try, try till you succeed,' the voice said. Rivanah picked up the bulb cursing herself for thinking she was smarter than the Stranger.

'What do you want?' she said.

'I'm happy for you. Finally you are getting where I always wanted you to.'

'Do you mean I'm close to finding the link between me and Hiya?'

'I only say things. What I mean depends on how smartly you interpret my words, Mini.'

'And when am I going to—' Rivanah stopped as her phone flashed 'Nivan calling'. She silenced the call and continued, 'When will I see who you really are?'

'Trust me, knowing my identity isn't going to help you in any way.'

'Would it hurt you if I get to know you?'

'Maybe.'

'But this is unfair,' Rivanah said. She waited for a response but there was none. *Is he gone?* Rivanah took a few unsure steps towards the water tank and then walked more confidently. But there was no sign of him. She was about to turn to leave when the Stranger leapt out of the darkness and held her tightly from behind so she had her back to him, pressing her mouth with one hand while grabbing both her wrists with another. She tried to free herself but he was too strong for her. Using his thumb and index finger of the hand which was pressing her mouth he clipped her nose. Her entire body was trying to break free but in vain. He appeared to be enjoying the fact that she was growing more and more breathless by the second. Her resistance became even stronger, and she knew that if she didn't breathe in the next five to ten seconds, she would die. A mental countdown had begun. And just when it reached 1, the Stranger released her. She inhaled as much oxygen as she could while the Stranger whispered in her ears, 'Remember this experience, Mini. I'll tell you later why.'

As he released her, Rivanah sat down on her knees trying to catch her breath. She wanted to look for the Stranger but felt stifled. She was sure the Stranger had disappeared by then. Her phone once again flashed 'Nivan calling'. She picked up.

'Hey, did you get through to your friend?'

'Yes.' She was still gasping for air.

'What happened?' Nivan sounded concerned.

'He was here.'

'What? Are you all right?'

'Now I am. Don't worry.'

'What did he say?'

'He knows what we are looking for.'

'We? He said that?'

'No. He meant me, but I'm sure he knows.' Rivanah finally stood up.

'I'm sure too.'

'Ishita will meet us tomorrow morning. I'll message you the address.'

'Okay. I'll wait. You take care. See you.'

Rivanah heard her mother calling her downstairs. 'Mini, what are you doing on the terrace?'

'Mumma, a bulb on the terrace has fused. We need to replace it,' Rivanah said and went downstairs, the Stranger's last words still echoing in her mind: *I will tell you later why.*

Next morning, Rivanah and Nivan took a cab to the CCD where Ishita was already waiting for her.

'It's lovely to see you, babes.' Ishita hugged Rivanah immediately and then went slightly stiff seeing Nivan.

'Tell me he is your cousin and is here to bride-hunt,' Ishita whispered in Rivanah's ears. The latter broke the hug with an amused face and said, 'Ishita, meet Nivan, my senior at work.' The two shook hands. As Nivan sat down, he realized the girls were still standing. He excused himself and stood back up.

'Please excuse us,' Rivanah said as Ishita pulled her towards the washroom. The moment they entered, Ishita asked, 'Is he your—'

'No! Though I didn't tell you I'm single now.'

'You are fucking Nivan?'

'Shut up, no!'

'What happened with Danny?'

'Same thing that happened with Ekansh. Life! We broke up because of my alleged infidelity.'

'What the fuck! Seriously?'

Rivanah nodded.

'And what exactly is Nivan doing here with you?'

Rivanah took two minutes to fill her in.

'Hmm. Everything is so twisted. Do give me your kundali after this.'

'Huh?'

'I want to know what kind of planetary position a girl needs to first have a hot guy like Danny and now a sex god.'

Rivanah smirked and with a tinge of sarcasm in her voice said, 'Oh, I too want to know that because every one of them slips out of my grasp.'

The girls came out of the washroom. They ordered their coffee after which Rivanah put it straight to Ishita, 'Just tell us what happened after we returned from Hiya's house last time.'

'Okay.' Ishita took a deep breath as if she was recollecting all of it correctly in her mind and then said, 'Your mother called a few times after which you said you had to accompany your parents to meet one of your father's colleagues. We guessed they wanted you and this colleague's son to get hitched. Then I guess you went there. I went with my colleagues for an outing where there was no phone network. I came back two days later, and when I called you back seeing your missed call alert and inquired if you had unearthed something about Hiya, you surprised the shit out of me by asking who Hiya was.'

Nivan glanced at Rivanah once and then looking at Ishita said, 'That's weird. How can Rivanah forget someone just like that?'

'This isn't the only weird thing that happened. I was pretty sure I had accompanied my parents to Mr Dutta's house.'

'Obviously, the two are connected. But how?' A couple of seconds later, Nivan asked, 'Who exactly is this Mr Dutta?'

'Manick Dutta is Baba's colleague.'

'Have you met him before?' Ishita asked.

'No.'

'And what exactly happened at his place? Do you remember?' Nivan asked.

'I went there, talked to him, all the while feeling sleepy. Then he suggested I take a nap. I was reluctant but my mother insisted as well. So I went to his bedroom only to doze off. And when I woke up, I was in my bedroom. Later, when I asked Baba, he said we were supposed to go to Mr Dutta's place but it was cancelled at the last moment.'

'You are scaring me,' Ishita said. They became quiet. Ishita's phone broke the silence. She took the call and, a few seconds later, told Rivanah, 'I'm sorry, but I have to go to office now. I'll call the moment I'm free today. Take care.' Ishita stood up.

'It was nice meeting you, Nivan,' she added, before hurrying out.

'We can trust Ishita, right?' Nivan asked.

'Oh yes. She knows everything.'

'Hmm. We have to pursue this mysterious Mr Dutta you mentioned.'

'I had messaged him on my father's behalf. And he asked if I was all right.'

'All right? You ask that if someone has had an accident or . . . if they are suffering from something.'

Rivanah had no clue what to say.

'Tell me something,' Nivan said, 'Is there anyone who might know everything about you for, let's say, a week, before and after Hiya's death? Not your parents. Like someone who was always there with you in college as well.'

Rivanah didn't have to think hard for this one. The name was clear in front of her: Ekansh Tripathi. How many times would she promise herself not to go to Ekansh and how many times would she have to break it?

27

The next morning, Rivanah considered several times before calling up Ekansh. She had blocked him, deleted his number and yet he kept reappearing in her life like an unwanted necessity. It showed her just how much their past was intertwined. And there was no way she could undo it. *The best way*, Rivanah decided, *was to pretend there was no past.* Holding on to this thought, she typed Ekansh's number on her dialler and called him. She would finish it over phone and be done with it.

The number you have called has been temporarily suspended, an automated voice said in Marathi.

What the fuck, Rivanah lamented. She typed a message, both on WhatsApp and SMS, and sent them to his number, hoping he read it. Morning turned to afternoon with no response from Ekansh. In the evening, Nivan called her.

Rivanah told him about Ekansh Tripathi, and Nivan enquired if he was the same person who had stayed in his flat before her. When she replied in the affirmative, it piqued Nivan's interest immediately. And he was sure

Ekansh would prove to be an asset in their quest though Rivanah tried to convince him he was nothing but an ass.

'Did you get through to him?'

'Not yet. His phone is temporarily suspended.'

'And there's no other way of getting in touch with him?'

'There is . . .' Rivanah knew she could call Ekansh's parents and get in touch with him. *But . . .*

'Did you try the alternative way?'

Rivanah wanted to say she wasn't interested, but Nivan didn't know of her past with Ekansh except for the fact he had been a good friend in college. And there was no reason why he should know anything else now.

'Give me two minutes. I'll call you back,' Rivanah said and cut the line. She remembered Ekansh's landline number as well. She cursed herself for remembering every inconsequential thing about him. *Perhaps girls are like that*, she concluded, *they remember the so-called unimportant details of a relationship much more than guys do*. She called on the landline which was answered on the fourth ring.

'Hello aunty, this is Rivanah here.'

The response came after a long pause, 'Hello, Rivanah.'

'I wasn't able to get through to Ekansh. Do you have any number where I can reach him? It's important.'

Rivanah heard Ekansh's mother move away from the receiver and call out to Ekansh.

'Hello?'

'Ekansh?'

'Rivanah?'

'What the hell are you doing in Kolkata?' she asked, and knew how weird it sounded. *He could be in Timbuktu, for God's sake. How does it matter?*

'I left my job.'

'Oh!'

'Where are you? How come you are calling me on my landline?'

'I'm in Kolkata. I called you on your Mumbai number but—'

'Yeah, I cancelled that number. Do you want to meet up?'

No, I want to finish it on phone, she thought but said, 'Okay, we'll keep it short.'

'If you want it short, it will be short.'

Why is he suddenly so friendly? Especially after the frivolous treatment she had been giving him?

'Coffee house?' he asked.

'Okay. In an hour.'

'Done.'

Rivanah cut the line and messaged Nivan saying she was meeting Ekansh shortly and would call Nivan once done.

Rivanah reached the Coffee House on time; Ekansh was already there. Was it a coincidence that he had chosen the same corner where they sat whenever they bunked college? She gave him a tight smile before sitting down opposite him.

'How is everything between Danny and you?' Ekansh asked.

Rivanah looked around and said, 'All's fine.' She wasn't going to give him a reason to feel he had a space in her life.

'Good,' he said.

She could sense sadness in his voice.

'I left my job and Mumbai too. I'll be at home for some time, figure out what I really want to do in life and then perhaps . . .'

'Hmm. That's nice.'

'I miss Tista.'

Rivanah had decided she wouldn't let him use his guilt as bait to fish her guilt out. She intentionally pretended his last sentence didn't mean much to her.

'I want you to tell me something, Ekansh. And tell me honestly.'

'Is that why we are meeting now?'

'Yes.'

'Okay, tell me, what is it?'

'You remember Hiya Chowdhury?'

He thought for a second and said, 'Yes, I do. You have asked me about her earlier too.'

'I know. She hanged herself a day before Tech Sky came to recruit on campus.'

'I remember that too.'

'I want you to tell me if you noticed anything odd about me from that day onwards.'

'Odd?' Ekansh seemed lost in thoughts. He spoke after some time, 'I think all was normal. You had gone on a vacation with your family for a month or so.'

'A month? Where?'

'What do you mean where? It was Leh and Ladakh, don't you remember?'

Leh and Ladakh. Rivanah had never seen any photographs of that vacation nor had any memory of it. Assuming she had made it to the vacation in the first place.

'Did I ever show you any pictures?'

Ekansh frowned and said, 'Why are you talking like you are an amnesia patient?'

Rivanah didn't react.

'I asked you for pictures, but you never showed me any,' Ekansh said.

'So, I was away for a month and then I was back and everything was normal?'

'You only went with your family for a vacation. It is normal anyway.'

Rivanah was thoughtful.

'Were we in touch when I was in Leh and Ladakh?'

'There was no network in your phone.'

'Which means we were out of touch.'

'Totally.'

Neither spoke for some time. Rivanah tried to fit in the information Ekansh had given her with whatever she knew of Hiya, but it didn't make sense: Hiya's death and her vacation—two seemingly unrelated incidents. *So many students must have gone on vacations at that time. So what?* But what kept her suspicions alive was the fact she didn't remember the vacation.

Ekansh snapped a finger to break Rivanah's trance. 'I think you are hiding something.'

Rivanah gave him a sharp glance and said, 'It's nothing. Thanks, Ekansh, for meeting up. I'll have to leave now.' She stood up. Ekansh grasped her hand rather impulsively. They looked into each other's eyes. Hers seemed to ask why and his why not. He let go of the grasp and asked, 'How long are you here in Kolkata?'

'I'm flying to Mumbai later tonight,' she lied and added genuinely, 'Stay well and take care. I miss Tista too.' Rivanah put her bag over her shoulder and walked off.

Nivan had been putting up in room no. 510 at the ITC Sonar Bangla. And though he had asked her if she wanted to meet outside, it was Rivanah who told him she wanted to be away from the noise and people for some time. She needed a quiet place to analyse the dots now that Ekansh had given her a new one—her supposed Leh and Ladakh family vacation.

'You want a tablet?' Nivan asked, noticing Rivanah rubbing her forehead as she settled on the couch in his suite.

'Perhaps some water,' she said.

Nivan brought her a bottle of water from the mini fridge.

'Thanks,' she said, taking a sip.

'What did Ekansh tell you?'

Rivanah took a minute to recount everything.

'So according to him, you tagged along with your parents to Leh and Ladakh, but you say you have no memory of it nor photographs to support it.'

'That's correct. Nor have I heard my parents ever mention it.'

'And you are confident Ekansh won't lie to you?'

Rivanah looked at Nivan. 'Why would he?'

'Okay. So after Ekansh, the two parties whom we should approach are Mr Dutta and—'

'And?'

'Hiya's parents. I remember. Ishita mentioned you two had gone to her place after the convocation.'

The mention of Hiya's parents brought back memories of the crazy-looking woman she had seen at her place and Hiya's worried-looking father. And yet she had forgotten only about Hiya and not her parents. *What. The. Fuck.*

'By comparing what Ekansh, Mr Dutta and Hiya's parents tell us, we can hope to get a solid lead.'

'Right.' Rivanah understood Nivan had a point. Nivan's phone, kept at the centre of the glass table, rang and vibrated at the same time. The vibration swirled the phone towards her. Before Nivan could pick it up,

Rivanah saw the name—Advika. Nivan excused himself and went to the other end of the room where the window was. As he stood there talking over the phone, Rivanah already had her questions ready for him. Nivan came back a couple of minutes later.

'Who is Advika?' she asked.

Nivan paused before settling on the couch again.

'I'm sorry if I'm being too personal,' she said.

'Advika is my girlfriend.'

'That's nice to know,' Rivanah said, knowing well Nivan must have guessed from her tone that she meant the opposite.

'What happened to her?' She had to ask something before the air turned too awkward between them.

Nivan reclined on the couch and set his gaze on the ceiling.

'Remember you asked me if I had a secret?'

Which you didn't tell me, Rivanah remembered clearly. 'Yes,' she said.

'Advika and I dated for five years and have been living together for seven.' Nivan was still staring at the ceiling. 'We met for the first time at a friend's birthday party after my higher-secondary exams. She had just passed her high school then. I remember she simply stood in one corner with a smile, not knowing I had my eyes on her all the time. I found her quietness amidst the party cacophony so very attractive. I can never forget that face . . . that moment. That evening, something unprecedented happened: I fell for a girl for the first time in my life. And it led me to do something I had never done before. I proposed to her by the time the party ended. She was so scandalized that she simple scampered away without saying anything. I became the butt of my friends' jokes. Then two days later, Advika got my number from a common friend and said yes to me on the phone. I never asked her why she took two days' time. All she told me was that, for her, I was the first. And I hope she knows that, for me, she is the last.' Nivan had a nostalgic smile on his face.

'Advika was always a non-confronting kind of girl, never found faults in others. It always surprised me. Actually, she'd always lived a protected life, never facing the harsh world ever, which ensured she had a pure heart. But it was not a practical one. During her college days, I used to pick her up from her house every day. The way she held on to me tightly every time I raced my bike amused me. And I did it on purpose most of the times.' The nostalgic smile on his face stretched at this point. He stood up and went to pick up his wallet from the table beside the television. He flipped it open, and staring at something inside said, 'Every touch of yours is a memory, each memory is an orgasm, each orgasm hides a realization and the realizations leads me to self-discovery.' He closed the wallet and came back to where he was sitting.

'It was something she had written for me after our first year together. I have kept it with me ever since. You know what, if I have to tell you about Advika in one line, she is a girl who never lost her innocence.'

Rivanah felt like she was hearing an excerpt from a romance novel. It sounded incredible and yet it urged Rivanah to believe it with her heart. The depth of a man's love, she realized while listening to Nivan, was evident in the way he reminisces about his girl.

'Advika was afraid of speed. She would never sit on a roller coaster. She always took her own sweet time to cross a busy road. Every time we took a flight, she would clasp my hand hard before take-off and while landing. That was also why she never learnt driving. I used to tease her about it, because speed was something that gave me a kick. Though I used to push her to learn driving, which she eventually did, Advika never really drove.' There was a pause akin to the one which usually preceded a storm.

'It was the fourteenth of April four years back, when we had planned to go for a movie at night. I was at work, and I had not brought my car that day. So, for a change, I wanted her to come over to the office and pick me up. She kept telling me we could take a cab, but I was adamant. After all, if one doesn't drive then how does one overcome this fear? I simply wanted her to confront her fear.' Nivan was suddenly quiet.

'And?'

Nivan's eyes fell upon Rivanah but he looked away quickly.

'She gave in to my stubbornness, drove but, before she could reach my office, met with an accident. A drunkard had hit her car. She injured her spine. The result of it,' his voice turned heavy as he completed, 'is for you to see.'

Rivanah was at a loss for words. There was a prolonged silence.

'I'm not going to marry her,' Nivan said, sounding choked.

Rivanah frowned.

'If I marry her,' he continued, 'People will make me believe that I'm with Advika because she is my responsibility. It would be my duty as a husband to be by her side. But, to be honest, Advika is neither my responsibility nor my duty. Advika is my choice. And when you choose someone, you are by default embracing all the consequences the choice may bring along.'

Rivanah tried to understand what Nivan was telling her, putting her life in context. Here was a man whose conviction in his love was so strong that it eclipsed the impossibility of it going the distance. Of course, Advika was an invalid now in every sense of the word, and yet this man sitting in front of Rivanah was confident of spending a lifetime with her. As if the tryst of destiny couldn't touch his love. As if fate was irrelevant. The realization of the existence of such a powerful love story made her feel empty. It made her feel jealous of Advika. And it made her feel insignificant too. She always wanted to be one such *choice* of one such *man*— neither responsibility nor duty, as Nivan had put it. She was happy to know such men existed, but they were the rarest of rare. And the one sitting in front of her was already taken.

'Life's unpredictable,' Nivan said, 'but if you don't stand by your choice, it will become incorrigible too. That's what the Stranger told me once.' He looked at Rivanah who was blank.

'What happened?'

Rivanah shook her head and said, 'I think I'll go home. Let's catch up tomorrow. I shall ask Ishita to join us.'

'All right.' Nivan looked thoughtful.

Rivanah took a cab. She was feeling dazed. Never before had she coveted someone's life like she now coveted Advika's. She felt an unprecedented urge to snatch Nivan away from her, to cast an evil spell so Nivan would get lured to her, would make her his choice, and make her feel everything that he made Advika feel.

With that one confession, Nivan had raised her expectations of men. When Danny broke up with her, he had given her reasons to abhor men and think of them as beings who would never understand the complexity of a woman. But Nivan pushed those reasons into insignificance and convinced her in no time to still be hopeful in a hopeless way. And it was the worst space to be in—to see someone like a horizon, visible but not attainable. What is it which decides who deserves whom? On the verge of having an emotional breakdown, Rivanah messaged the Stranger:

I seriously need to talk. Please tell me you are there.

A few seconds later the Stranger replied:

At your house, Mini?

Rivanah made a mad dash for her house.

28

Rivanah called up her parents on the way, fearing their life may be in danger. But they both were in New Market, shopping. They told her they would be back by evening, and asked her to take the spare key from their neighbour. Rivanah didn't let them get a whiff of her anxiety. The cab dropped her right in front of her house, and she went to the neighbour to collect the spare key. The neighbour wanted to chat, but Rivanah cut her short and walked up to the main door of her house and, looking around, slowly unlocked it. She peeped in first and then stepped in. She could smell Just Different by Hugo Boss in the air.

'You there?' The drawing room was filled with darkness since all the curtains, she noticed, were drawn. She had never been so scared to enter her own house before.

'Close the door, Mini,' a voice commanded.

Rivanah shut the door behind her trying to identify where the voice had come from.

'Take a seat.'

Now she knew where the voice was coming from. Behind the refrigerator, she could see the silhouette of the upper half of someone's head as the head rested on folded hands atop the refrigerator. The Stranger's figure was hidden by the refrigerator. Rivanah didn't move for some time, while calculating what her next move should be.

'Take a seat, Mini,' the Stranger repeated. She went to the sofa and saw a blindfold and a handcuff on it. She knew what was expected of her, but was it necessary? She was about to object when she heard him speak again.

'You move, I move out. You shout or run, you lose me. You don't listen to me, this meeting is over.'

Damn you, she thought and put on the blindfold first and then locked her hands with the handcuff.

'Happy?' she said.

'More than ever, Mini. Tell me, what do you want to talk about?'

'I'll be honest. Nivan told me how you were after him like the way you have been after me.'

'I guessed that.'

'Nivan also confessed to me about Advika.'

'So?'

'It made me realize that deep down I have always desired a man like Nivan. He is the personification of my idea of *the* man. Also, until today, I always thought I deserved a man like this. But do I really deserve someone like Nivan? If not, then why not? I want to know my flaw and rectify it because I'm sick and tired of the hypocrite men I have had in my life. One more and I'll kill him.' Her angst mixed with envy made the Stranger smile.

'Do we deserve someone or not is a question that can't be answered. It's essentially a rhetorical question. But what can be answered is why you had the ones you had.'

'Why did I have Ekansh? Why did I fall for Danny?'

'Just like you were meant to love them genuinely, Ekansh and Danny were not meant to understand that genuineness of yours. Have you ever thought of looking at it this way: both Ekansh and Danny probably weren't meant to be in a committed relationship with you? Maybe it was your misinterpretation of it. Whoever comes in and walks out of our life always has a role to perform. We simply don't see it that way. Ekansh's and Danny's roles were to make you realize that people may claim they love you, but at certain moments of truth, it is proved that their love is superficial. Nivan's role is to make you not give up on love in the first place.'

'Will I be a bad girl if I tell you I want Nivan, knowing well he is committed for life? I know it started with him being a silly crush of mine, but today he has shaken my core. I feel like I have wasted my life seeking the kind of love Nivan has for Advika in Ekansh and Danny.'

The Stranger was quiet as Rivanah tried wiping the tears from under the blindfold with her handcuffed hands.

'Why are you sad, Mini?'

'I'm sad because after all this time that you have been asking me to know my worth—and I have probably known my worth to some extent—it still doesn't make me eligible enough to deserve Nivan.'

'You know, Mini, the toughest kind of acceptance is when we have to accept that there are certain things in life which can't be ours—no matter how hard we try. It's called growing up, Mini. It's difficult—very, very difficult, but inevitable nevertheless. Worse, growing up doesn't only happen as we turn eighteen. Growing up happens as our soul keeps swallowing these depressing acceptances little by little, one at a time. For no acceptance can happen overnight. It's a bit-by-bit process. The way a patient is given saline. If you try to accept the fact that Nivan can't be yours right at this moment, you will destroy yourself further.'

Neither spoke for a long time. Rivanah took her time to get a grip on her emotional self.

She felt a hand cupping her face. She sensed the Stranger was standing right beside her.

'The surgery will soon be over. And any surgery without anaesthesia will cause pain. Just hold on for some more time, Mini. It'll all be worth it. Trust me.' His words made no sense to Rivanah.

'What do you mean?' Rivanah said, looking up. She felt something being thrust in her hand. It was the key to the handcuff. She immediately unlocked herself, removed the blindfold to see an empty drawing room. The curtains had been drawn open and there was light pouring in.

The doorbell rang. Her parents had come back. She quickly stood up and shoved the blindfold and the handcuff into an empty drawer nearby. Her parents had purchased some clothes for her from New Market, but she wasn't interested in trying them out. Making an excuse of missing old times, Rivanah opened all the family photo albums, but found no pictures from her Leh—Ladakh trip. She couldn't ask her parents about it, now that she was slowly beginning to understand there was indeed something they were hiding from her. In the evening, she called Ishita and told her to keep herself free the next day. They would have to visit Hiya's place again.

The next day Rivanah accompanied Ishita and Nivan to Hiya's place in Agarpara. Nivan insisted only Ishita accompany him. Since they didn't know yet how Rivanah and Hiya were connected, it was better—or so Nivan thought—to keep Rivanah away from Hiya's parents.

As the two went inside, Rivanah went to a tea stall nearby and waited for them there. They came out after an hour. Rivanah strode across the road to them the moment they came out of Hiya's house.

'What happened?'

'Hiya Chowdhury had a little brother as well,' Ishita said, gloomily.

'How is he related to me?' Rivanah asked, looking at Ishita and then at Nivan.

'Let's talk in the car,' he said.

Ishita sat quietly sitting with Rivanah in the back seat of the car they had come in, while Nivan sat beside the driver. They all were silent until Rivanah chose to speak.

'What happened? What about the little brother?'

'Hiya's little brother had some kidney problem for which he needed dialysis. Her father had exhausted every bit of his savings on it, and Hiya's getting into Tech Sky was their only hope of continuing with the dialysis,' Nivan said.

'So that's why she hanged herself?' Rivanah asked.

'We don't know that yet. Mr Chowdhury showed us the pieces of white cloth Hiya had received, which means the Stranger was behind her as well. Whether he pushed her to hang herself or she did it on her own discretion is hard to say.'

Rivanah knew that any conclusion about the Stranger would be useless. His last words though—*the surgery is about to get over soon*—sounded dangerously loaded.

'Now only the third link is left—Mr Dutta,' Nivan said.

'Do we approach him today?' Ishita asked.

'Today itself,' Nivan said, and turned to look at Rivanah, 'Did you do it?'

Before going to bed the previous night, Nivan had asked Rivanah to message Mr Dutta from her father's phone and fix an appointment somewhere outside, as if it was her father who wanted to meet him. Rivanah did what was asked of her.

'Mr Dutta will meet my father at 3 p.m. at Mio Amore in Russel Street.'

'Your father?' Ishita was surprised.

'For Mr Dutta, it is my father meeting him,' Rivanah said. Ishita understood.

They reached Mio Amore before time. Nivan and Ishita took a table, and Rivanah sat at another, with her back to the entrance. Her presence would be announced only when the time was right.

Mr Dutta reached the place shortly after three. He took a table and told the waiter that he was waiting for a friend and would place his order once the friend arrived. Nivan, who kept an eye on every single man entering the place, worked on his instinct as he stood up and went to Mr Dutta.

'Mr Dutta, isn't it?'

'Yes?' Mr Dutta looked up at Nivan.

'Hi, I am Nivan.' He shook hands with him. This was a cue for Ishita to join them.

'What is this about?' Mr Dutta asked, feeling slightly uncomfortable.

'This is about a friend of ours,' Nivan said, taking a seat and helping Ishita to settle down beside him.

'Which friend?'

'Rivanah Bannerjee.'

For a moment, Mr Dutta seemed slightly taken aback but he quickly regained composure.

'I still don't understand this.'

'I'm sure you remember me, uncle?' It was Rivanah who stood up from the table nearby and joined the lot.

'We don't mean any harm,' Nivan clarified. 'We just want to know what happened the day Rivanah visited you with her parents.'

'But I'm not supposed to divulge information related to my patients to anyone,' Mr Dutta said, and immediately knew he had given a hint already.

'Patients?' Rivanah frowned.

'Mr Dutta, if Rivanah is your patient, then you don't have the right to hide anything from her, at least. Am I right?' Nivan said.

Mr Dutta understood they wouldn't take anything short of the truth. He drank some water from the glass in front of him, and said, 'Okay, I'll tell you everything. I knew it had to come out one day. But will you be able to handle it?' He was looking at Rivanah.

29

'I don't have a choice any more, uncle. Nobody can escape their own story, can they?' Rivanah appeared calm.

Mr Dutta seemed to understand what she meant. All three were waiting for him to speak.

'Rivanah was brought to me by her parents almost a year and a half ago,' Mr Dutta said, 'I could see it in her eyes then that she needed medical treatment. But her parents said they were done with medicine and doctors. Her mother especially was hysterical about losing her daughter. She had heard about me from a distant relative, I think. I calmed her down before focussing on Rivanah. She was acutely restless and seemed like she hadn't slept in a long time. The kind of profession I'm in, I get all kinds of patients, but looking at Rivanah I realized she was more a victim of acute remorse, more than anything else. At first I had to calm her down to know exactly what the problem was. All she kept repeating was "I killed someone".'

Rivanah swallowed. She knew Ishita had glanced at her but she was too shocked to return the glance. Nivan was calmly looking at Mr Dutta as the latter continued.

'I asked her whom have you killed and she took a name—Hiya Chowdhury. Her parents clarified that nothing of that sort had happened. Confused, I took her to my room, my work station, where I induced her into deep sleep through hypnosis.' Mr Dutta looked at Rivanah and said, 'I'm a professional hypnotist.'

There was a silence gravid with inquisitiveness.

'I understand your doubts. Hypnosis may not be talked about much socially, but a lot of people use it in their everyday life. A lot of my patients have used it to forgo labour pain during childbirth. Especially the ones who are adamant to go without a caesarean. Lot of patients also use hypnosis to counter guilt. Though I would agree that there are very few genuine hypnotists left.'

'What happened next, Mr Dutta?' Nivan asked.

'After the induction of deep sleep, Rivanah started talking to me, giving away whatever she had been hiding in her conscious and her subconscious self. I learned that Rivanah and Hiya were fierce competitors in college. In fact, Rivanah told me she'd never accepted it openly, but was actually jealous of Hiya for scoring higher than her in every semester examination. I remember I'd asked you to name one thing which irked you the most about Hiya. And you'd said it was her laughter. You thought it had a mocking tinge to it.'

Rivanah remembered how the Stranger had set Hiya's laughter as the doorbell sound.

'Over time, the jealousy turned into a grudge as if Hiya had deliberately scored higher to put Rivanah down—or so Rivanah came to believe. Belief isn't as simple a thing as we think it is. It can eclipse a lot of things from your sight. Anyway, the year in concern was different, since there were job cuts and economic slowdown all over, and only one IT MNC was scheduled to visit Rivanah's college campus—Tech Sky. The company was supposed to recruit ten students but not from one college. They were supposed to visit ten colleges and pick one student from each. There were protests against the recruitment manager but all of it came to nothing. Rivanah knew that if they could only select one candidate, it would be Hiya since she was the brightest in her batch. And she had to beat her once and for all to show who the best was.

'Two nights before, Rivanah bought some over-the-counter sleeping pills, searched on Google for the amount needed to make someone sleep for long but not kill, and experimented on herself. She had the pills at 8.30 p.m. and then woke up around 1 p.m. the next day, having slept like a log throughout. Her plan was convincing and would not raise any doubt. Do we blame someone if we oversleep suddenly one day? It was too casual a thing to seem suspicious—or so she thought. The night before Tech Sky was supposed to visit the college for recruitment, Rivanah was ready to implement her experiment for real.' Mr Dutta glanced at Rivanah. A teardrop rolled down her cheek. He averted his eyes to Nivan; he knew he wouldn't be able to continue otherwise.

'Rivanah called for a group study session to exchange notes at one of their batchmate's room in the college girl's hostel. There were four girls in total who met that night in the hostel room: Rivanah, Meera, Hiya and Pooja. The last one was Rivanah's best friend in college, or so I was told by her parents later. The four girls discussed possible questions for the impending interview until very late in the night, and next morning went to the college for the exam and interview. Except one—Hiya. She didn't wake up on time and was left behind in the hostel room. And by the time she woke up, Tech Sky had already selected their quota of one candidate from the college: Rivanah Bannerjee.'

Nobody spoke for a minute. Rivanah had her face half covered with a hand as if she might die if she saw anyone looking at her.

'What happened to Hiya?' Ishita asked.

'Hiya had overslept. Unknown to her, Rivanah had mixed sleeping pills in her coffee the night before; the same number of pills—not enough to kill her but make her sleep longer than desired. Rivanah's parents told me later that Hiya hanged herself to death. This was the trigger to Rivanah's emotional breakdown.'

'And what did you do to Rivanah? How come she never remembered all this?' Ishita asked.

'Something which I do only in rare and extreme cases. With deep hypnosis, one can push one's memories from the conscious to the deep subconscious. Some people call it erasing memory as well, but technically it's never totally erased. It is there in the subconscious and can manifest itself in the form of dreams.'

And nightmares . . . Rivanah thought but didn't say anything aloud.

'Because it's a part of you. Or sometimes it can also manifest itself in creative endeavours like writing or,' Mr Dutta glanced at Rivanah and continued, 'sketching.'

'You mean the sketches you drew were of . . .' Ishita said and saw Rivanah nodding gently.

'This was why your parents brought you to me the last time. They were petrified when they discovered you had sketched Hiya Chowdhury's face. They feared you would know the truth again and probably go berserk the way you had done for that one month. It was an emotionally taxing time not only for you, but your parents too.'

One month . . . when she was supposed to be on vacation to Leh and Ladakh with her parents . . . Rivanah was joining the dots in her mind.

'I had to push whatever you came to know about Hiya into your deep subconscious once again. That's why you forgot everything related to her quite abruptly,' Mr Dutta said. A waiter came and asked if they wanted to order anything. Mr Dutta shook his head and said to

Rivanah, 'But I have a question which I had asked your father too, but he had no answer. How come you knew about Hiya Chowdhury once again? I understand about the sketching, but what propelled you to realize there's a Hiya in the first place? I mean you are my only patient who has backtracked like this on my hypnosis. And, trust me, I have treated a lot of patients in the thirty years of my career.'

Rivanah glanced at Nivan to know if she should tell him about the Stranger.

'It was from a sketch which one of her friends identified as Hiya. It made her curious, one thing led to another and here we are.' Nivan quickly came to the rescue.

'Hmm. That's it?'

'That's it,' Nivan said conclusively.

Mr Dutta had nothing more to say. He took his leave, wishing Rivanah the best and offered his help if she needed it. Rivanah was as if in a trance, but did have a request for Mr Dutta.

'Please don't tell any of this to my parents,' she said.

'I won't, if you promise me you won't let whatever I told you break you.'

Rivanah nodded. How much further could she break? She went out with Nivan and Ishita to where the car was waiting for them.

'I'll have to leave you guys here since my boss needs me in office,' said Ishita

'We can drop you,' Nivan said.

'I think Rivanah needs to be home now,' Ishita said. Nivan agreed. Ishita hugged Rivanah but the latter didn't feel the hug.

'Be strong. What has happened has happened. We all commit mistakes. I'll be in touch.' Ishita went away towards an auto. Both Nivan and Rivanah climbed into their cab. The driver was asked to take them to Rivanah's place.

'No. The hotel,' she said. Nivan gave her a short glance and then nodded at the driver.

It was a quiet drive. Rivanah took Nivan's hand in hers, surprising him. While looking out of the window, away from Nivan, she started sobbing profusely. Nivan immediately asked the driver to park the car in a lonely lane. The driver was asked to wait outside the car. The moment the driver locked the door, Rivanah turned to look at Nivan.

'How can I be such a bitch?' she said. 'Just to show I was the best, I ended up taking someone's life?'

'You didn't intend to take her life. You wanted to secure a job for yourself.' A pause later he added, 'Just like I wanted Advika to conquer her fear and pick me up that night.' Nivan sighed and said, 'I too didn't intend her to become an invalid for the rest of her life.'

With teary eyes she looked up at Nivan and said, 'Even if I hadn't planned to kill Hiya, I had spiked her coffee in a cold-blooded manner. I was the trigger.'

'It's unbelievable how a seemingly small decision of ours can proliferate into our worst nightmare.'

'Did she really kill herself because she couldn't get the job?'

'I've a feeling this is only half the story.'

'Who would tell us the other half?' Rivanah shot an inquiring look at him.

'The one who pushed you to this half,' Nivan said. And she knew whom Nivan was hinting at.

30

It was a quiet drive to the hotel. The revelations had left Rivanah speechless. How do you accept such an acidic self of yours that you didn't even know existed so far? There was a cold-blooded killer buried inside her. With this realization she had lost the right to question anyone on anything. Ekansh had only ditched her, Danny had only misunderstood her, but she had pushed someone to commit suicide, however unintentional it may be.

As she walked inside the room with Nivan, he received a phone call. Rivanah heard him talk to Advika and learnt he was flying to Mumbai later that night. Once the call ended Nivan came to Rivanah who had quietly settled on the couch seemingly withdrawn.

'I'll have to fly back in some hours. Advika needs me.'

Rivanah needs me . . . will someone ever say that? Rivanah wondered. And answered her own question: why would someone? Now she knew why she could never deserve a man like Nivan. She deserved whatever had happened to her so far and she had no right to find solace in cribbing.

'Rivanah? You all right?' Nivan asked.

'Yeah.' Both she and Nivan knew she was anything but all right.

'If you need more leaves from office, let me know. I'll talk to the management.'

'I think I will be coming to Mumbai shortly as well.'

'To be honest, I think that would help you to move on as quickly as possible.'

Move on from what? The ugly person that I am? Won't I forever carry the person within me? She asked, 'What did you do when you learnt Advika paid the price of your stubbornness?'

'Though whatever happened to Advika was unintended, I still believe it happened because of my stubbornness. Advika may have become invalid, but Arun died.'

'Arun?' Somewhere the name rang a bell for Rivanah.

'Arun Rawat. He was the one who crashed his car into Advika's.'

Rivanah now knew where she had heard the name. Arun was the son of Dilip Rawat, the one for whom the Stranger had made her sign the cheque from the last bit of her savings once. *Was everything always connected?*

'I knew it would be difficult not to break bit by bit everyday seeing Advika in her present condition, but I was made to realize that if I broke down completely, so would Advika and whatever was left of us. And "us" was everything I ever had. "Us" was something I could compromise my life for.'

'You were made to realize?'

'By the Stranger. He helped me realize a bad stubborn choice may define us momentarily. Unfortunately, most of us have this bad habit of wasting the whole because of the momentary.'

'But the momentary choice ended up taking a life.'

'In my case too it ended up taking two lives. Arun was dead.'

'And the second life?'

'The life Advika and I would have lived had I not pushed her to drive that night.'

In that case, I've taken two lives as well, Hiya, and the life she would have lived if I hadn't mixed the pills in the coffee, Rivanah thought.

Nivan called the reception. He told them he would check out in some time and asked the receptionist to be ready with the necessary bills. Then he called someone and asked them to book a business class ticket for the next flight to Mumbai. As he finished the call, Nivan said, 'We are still assuming Hiya killed herself because of you. Maybe there's something that we don't know yet. I still feel it's half the story. And half stories often lead us to wrong inference.'

'Maybe,' she said.

There was silence. Rivanah knew she had to leave, so Nivan could pack up. But she felt too heavy to move. How could she face her parents now that she knew what they were hiding from her?

There was a momentary eye lock between Nivan and Rivanah. The moment it happened, she didn't know why she blurted out, 'May I please hug you once?'

Nivan looked at her and came forward. She stood up and hugged him with such tightness that it took Nivan by surprise, though he didn't say anything. Rivanah knew it wasn't a friendly hug—it was more, it had passion in it and a claim but she couldn't help it. The hug didn't seem like a first. Rivanah wanted Nivan to understand her unsaid claim, the way an author wants his readers to understand the unwritten. She would have prolonged the hug had Nivan's phone not rung.

'Excuse me,' he said and broke the hug. Before he took the call, she said, 'I'll see you in Mumbai. Thanks for all the support.' She left the hotel room.

Once home, Rivanah tried to be normal the way her parents did even after knowing they had made her forget that one fact which could have altered her life. She would do the same. Not let them realize she knew what they were hiding. Rivanah surprised herself with how normally she was behaving, even though she wasn't looking straight at either of them. With a blank mind, she kept watching television, talked to Ishita for some time keeping her responses simple. Ishita understood she needed some alone time on this. Rivanah booked her ticket to Mumbai and then had her dinner with her parents, pretending all was fine. The pretence scared her and also relaxed her at the same time.

Lying on her bed at night, she messaged the Stranger: *You there?*

For a change the Stranger didn't respond immediately.

A message from a new number popped up: *Can we meet for coffee once more?*

She checked the display picture and noticed Tista and Ekansh together.

I told you I'm in Mumbai, Rivanah replied.

I too am in Mumbai. Serving notice period for two months.

I'll let you know.

She saw Ekansh typing but she received no message. She didn't probe either. Waiting for the Stranger's reply, she scrolled down to Nivan's name on her WhatsApp contact list. She tapped on his display picture and kept staring at it for some time, after which she messaged him: *Reached?*

She received a reply soon enough: *Yes, I did. How are you now?*

I'm okay. I've booked a flight to Mumbai tomorrow.

Good. Any intimation from the Stranger yet?

Not yet. I messaged but no reply yet.

Okay. Keep me updated. See you soon.

Sure, see you.

After thinking for few seconds she typed: *May I tell you something?*

Sure. Nivan messaged back.

Rivanah typed: *I love you, Nivan. Not like the way one usually desires someone. My love won't limit you to choose between Advika or me. I'll only be limiting myself to you with my love. It won't attempt to own you either but only request you to make me a part, or perhaps an extension, of whatever you share with Advika. I'll be more than happy to hide myself within the shadow of your and Advika's relationship. I know it's weird but to be loved the way Advika is loved by you is perhaps my only redemption. It may sound selfish but—*

Rivanah paused for a moment and then deleted the entire message. She rewrote instead:

Nothing important really. Goodnight, Nivan.

31

Heading for the airport the next morning, Mrs Bannerjee was narrating to Rivanah what happened between her and Rivanah's maternal aunt.

'She was as usual being poky. All through the phone call, she was hinting that we have decided to make you sit at home all your life. She has shifted to the US but her mentality will never shift.'

Rivanah was facing the other way, not really paying attention to what her mother was telling her.

'I also told her my daughter is the best.'

Rivanah suddenly gave her a sharp look as she heard her mother say, 'And for the best, we have selected the best.' She looked at Rivanah and continued, 'I didn't take Nivan's name, but your father and I have decided that we will talk to him once you go to Mumbai. He is the best match for you.'

The last statement broke all her defences, and Rivanah started sobbing uncontrollably, holding her mother tight. Her father, who was driving the car, kept looking at his wife via the rear-view mirror, confused.

'What happened, Mini? Tell me.' Her worried mother egged her on, but Rivanah wasn't ready to speak. Her embrace only tightened. *I'm a bitch, Mumma. And I only deserve shit.* It was only when her father said if she didn't talk, he would drive her back to their house and cancel her Mumbai flight, that Rivanah said aloud, 'Nivan is committed.' It wasn't why she was crying, but then she wasn't sure why exactly she was crying. Mrs Bannerjee too had tears in her eyes as she glanced at her husband, understanding that their daughter perhaps had feelings for Nivan.

'It's okay, Mini. I'm sure there are other guys like Nivan.'

No, Baba. There is nobody like him. Nivan is rare. And to get to him, one had to be rarer. Like Advika. Not like me.

'I think you shouldn't go to Mumbai today,' Mr Bannerjee said

'No, Baba. I'll have to. I don't have any more leaves. I want to work to take my mind off other things.'

Mr Bannerjee agreed that work would be the right anodyne for his daughter and didn't speak any further.

Ishita was waiting for her at the departure gate as the Bannerjee family climbed down from the car. She came and hugged her friend tight.

'Everything will be all right,' Ishita whispered in her ears.

'Yeah.' Rivanah spoke softly.

'Go for Nivan. He is a good guy. I'm sure he will keep you happy,' Ishita whispered next. Though Rivanah had said nothing about her feelings for Nivan to her, Ishita had still understood it. Was Rivanah so obvious? Had Nivan too understood it as clearly and as correctly like Ishita did?

'He is committed,' she told Ishita. The latter broke the hug and looked deep into Rivanah's eyes. The kind of pain Ishita saw in them churned her guts. She hadn't seen it even when Ekansh had ditched her or when she had told her that Danny and she had broken up. It was the kind of pain which comes when someone's innocence is lost once and for all.

'You will be late, Mini,' Mr Bannerjee said.

'Be in touch,' Ishita said. Rivanah proceeded to the gate. She knew her parents were waiting for her to turn around and wave at them, but she didn't. She just couldn't.

The flight landed on time. She reached the Residency Enclave soon after. She glanced once at Nivan's door, as she was about to unlock her flat. But her door opened suddenly, and Rivanah saw Nivan's servant and Advika on her wheelchair inside her flat. Advika was smiling at her.

'Nivan told me you were coming, so we thought of dusting the flat a bit,' Advika said, her speech slurry.

How can she be so damn good to others? Rivanah thought, and said, 'That's really kind of you Advika.'

'You must be tired. I'll leave you now. We can catch up later.'

'Sure.'

'Is Nivan back?' Advika asked the servant. She nodded.

'Where is he?' Rivanah asked.

'He must be downstairs taking his karate class,' Advika said and took her leave. Rivanah watched them step out of her flat and then get into the adjacent flat, closing the door behind them. Rivanah immediately locked her flat and went downstairs. She didn't have to look for long before she found Nivan with a group of young girls in white martial-arts attire in a circle on the society ground. They were watching something. As Rivanah approached Nivan, he looked up and asked her to be quiet, gesturing her to look ahead. She did. A girl seemingly of her age was fighting a strong-looking guy. He was about to punch her but the girl flipped in a flash and kicked him on the face. The man lost his footing and fell down. Everyone clapped and cheered. Nivan had a smile on his face.

'What's this?' Rivanah asked.

'I'm a black belt in karate,' Nivan said. 'And I teach these girls the art of self-defence. He called it "share your good luck".'

The words took Rivanah back to her past when she taught ten slum kids—Mini's Magic 10.

'Hey Rivanah!' It was Smita from work.

'What are you doing here?' Rivanah asked.

'Joined here a few weeks ago.'

Rivanah remembered a pamphlet on her desk regarding some karate class. She did think about giving it a shot, but never knew it was managed by Nivan.

'All good at home?' Smita asked.

Rivanah nodded, shooting a furtive glance at Nivan.

'Great. See you in office,' Smita said and left.

'Can I be a part of it as well?' Rivanah asked.

'Sure. You don't even have to ask. From tomorrow morning?'

'From tomorrow morning,' she confirmed.

Together they went back into the building. At work, the first thing she did was to approach Argho.

'I wanted to apologize for whatever happened to you that day in the police station,' she said. Argho wasn't expecting her to apologize once again.

'It's okay. You'd already apologized the other day.'

'I know,' she said. *I wish I could tell you this apology is actually for something else. I can't face Hiya's parents, and you are her next family link I know of.*

'Did you find out who was playing games with you?'

'Not yet.'

'Let me know if you do.'

'Sure.'

The moment she was in her cubicle, she messaged the Stranger: *I need to talk. Where are you???*

The Stranger was yet to respond to her last message. She tried calling the numbers she had with her. All the ten numbers that she had of the Stranger produced the same result: *The number you are trying to reach has been withdrawn.*

Clouded by suspicion, Rivanah rushed to Nivan's cabin. Looking at her, he knew it was something urgent.

'What happened?'

'I think the Stranger won't contact me again. And I can't let that happen. I can't afford to lose him. Not now. Not ever.'

'How do you know he won't contact you?'

'None of his numbers are active any more. And he hasn't responded to my message in over twenty-four hours. This has never happened before.'

Reclining on his seat, Nivan looked thoughtful.

'You must have the Stranger's number?' Rivanah asked.

'I do. First come in and close the door,' he said.

Rivanah did as asked and said, 'Could you please dial him?'

Nivan picked up his phone from the table and opened Contacts. He scrolled down and reached the name which read Stranger. Placing his phone on the table again, he dialled the number. The screen flashed 'Calling Stranger'. He tapped on the speaker mode. Both Nivan and Rivanah could hear the rings. On the fifth ring, the phone was picked up.

'Hello,' the person at the other end of the line said.

It can't be, Rivanah thought. The voice belonged to someone dear to her once, someone acutely close to her, someone she loved, someone who had left her broken recently. Someone who also went by the name Danny.

32

Nivan tapped the mute button and asked, 'What happened?' He felt Rivanah had perhaps identified the voice. She didn't react though.

'Do you know the person?' he egged on.

Rivanah nodded. She was too shocked to talk. *Is Danny the Stranger? Both Nivan's and mine?*

'Hello?'

Danny was still on line. Nivan, who was still looking at Rivanah, tapped on the red button and the call ended.

'Is this the same voice who talks to you?' Nivan asked.

'No. But then it never was one voice throughout.'

'Same here. Sometimes it's a woman, sometimes an old man and sometimes a teenager. This time it's a man.'

A man who feigned Danny's voice? Or was it Danny himself? Rivanah said, 'Precisely. I'll wait till the Stranger contacts me.' She didn't feel comfortable mentioning Danny to Nivan—especially their shared past. The moment she left Nivan's cabin, she once again dialled all the numbers belonging to the Stranger. They were still not available. Frustrated, she checked her Contacts and realized she'd deleted Danny's number long back. She checked her Truecaller history and finally got Danny's number. She saved it under his name. On a hunch, she went back to Nivan's cabin.

'Could I please get the number you called for the Stranger? Just in case . . .'

'Sure.' Nivan called out the number. As she punched it in her dial pad, she thanked Nivan and stepped out to dial the number. Her phone's screen soon flashed 'Calling Danny'. The number which Nivan stored as 'Stranger' in his phone was in fact Danny's number. Going by the record, it could be a duplicate sim and a mimicked voice, but Rivanah knew she wouldn't be able to focus on anything till she was sure. The phone kept ringing and was finally picked up. *Is it because he still has my number and is in two minds seeing my name?* Rivanah wondered, and heard him say, 'Hi.'

'Hi ba—' Rivanah was about to say 'baby' but paused at the right moment. It was funny how relationships programmed a mind.

'What happened suddenly?' Danny said.

I'll have to meet him, she thought, but said, 'Congrats on the film thing.' She was already framing her next sentence in her mind as she heard him say, 'Thank you. I thought you would never call.'

'I thought you wouldn't pick up.'

'I thought you wouldn't think about me.'

'I thought you wouldn't talk to me.'

There was silence. Did Danny react the way he did because he wanted to leave her alone, because he indeed was the Stranger? Was his entire plan of coming into her life as a sexy neighbour an attempt to be close to her to know her every move? Why would he do that? And why would he behave the same with Nivan? *Things might clear up*, she thought, *if we met once*. Rivanah was praying Danny himself would mention the meeting part, as it was becoming tougher for her to say it aloud. Deep down, she knew even this time she didn't want to meet him because she was missing him, but she wanted to know if his phone really had received a call from Nivan.

'Listen, I'm shooting for a magazine. I'll have to go.'

'Can we meet for some time today?' Rivanah finally blurted out.

'Okay. I'll be with a friend in Boveda later in the evening.'

It was clear he didn't want to rekindle anything between them, or else he wouldn't be rude enough to meet her while he was meeting a friend.

'Sure.' Rivanah thought she too would make it clear she wasn't looking to go back into the past.

'Around eight,' Danny said.

Rivanah was late by half an hour due to heavy traffic. Before she could guide the cab driver to the place, she received an unexpected call.

'Is that Rivanah Bannerjee?'

'Speaking, who is it?'

'This is Inspector Kamble.'

It took few seconds for Rivanah to recollect who Inspector Kamble was.

'How are you, sir?'

'I'm good. How are you doing? Glad you remember.'

'I'm good too.'

'Listen, would it possible for you to come down to the Goregaon police station anytime soon.'

'Now?'

'Not now. But maybe tomorrow.'

'Sure, I will. But what happened?'

'There's something I want to talk to you about. Will tell you when we meet.'

'All right, sir.'

Rivanah remembered how worried Inspector Kamble used to be for his daughter, though the last time she met him, he had told her she had got a job in Mumbai itself. Rivanah guided the cab driver and reached Boveda soon. She entered to realize a karaoke night was in full swing. A guy and a girl were singing an Enrique song. It wasn't long before Rivanah's eyes located Danny. He was looking happier than ever before, talking to a girl. Danny's eyes spotted Rivanah as he stood up. She understood he didn't want her to come up to him. The girl with whom Danny was sitting had her back to Rivanah. She turned to flash a smile at her. It was Nitya. The sight of her was like a bullet through her heart. Did Danny intentionally call her there because he was meeting Nitya? Or did he meet Nitya because Rivanah wanted to meet him? Were Danny and Nitya in a relationship?

'Let's go outside. I need to smoke,' Danny said as he walked past Rivanah. He didn't even appreciate the fact that they were meeting after a long time. She was ready for a hug even if it was going to be awkward. She turned to follow Danny outside. He lit a cigarette.

'When did this happen?' Rivanah said. Seeing her glance at Nitya, Danny knew what she was talking about.

'Never you mind,' he said, looking around constantly, as if he thought someone was filming him.

For Rivanah, those three words were loaded enough to answer her query regarding Nitya's presence. They were seeing each other. A casual glance at Nitya told her she was smirking at her. I-finally-won-bitch kind of smirk. A slight anger nudged her, but Rivanah knew she didn't have the right to express it.

'What's up?' Danny said.

If he wants to keep it to the point, I shall keep it to the point, Rivanah decided and said, 'I want to see your phone's call list once.'

'What?'

'You heard me.'

'What for? And what makes you think you still have the right to check my phone?'

'I know I don't. That's why I am asking you. It's related to the Stranger,' she said and noticed Danny pause in between a puff, and then release the smoke at one go.

'I'm sorry, but I don't want to show you my phone.'

'Why not?'

Danny's hesitation persuaded Rivanah to believe her suspicions: Danny perhaps was the Stranger.

'A phone is a personal belonging.'

'I am not interested in your chats or pictures. All I want you to do is open your call history and show it to me. You don't have to give the phone to me.'

'Call history?'

'What's happening, baby?' It was Nitya.

'Nothing. She wants to see my call history.'

'You sure you haven't lost it, Rivanah?' Nitya said. It was quite insulting, but Rivanah didn't react.

'One glimpse, Danny, and I shall be forever gone.'

Danny and Nitya exchanged a glance. Nitya took Danny's phone and unlocked it. The fact that Rivanah never knew Danny's password made her feel inferior. But it was momentary. Nitya held the phone flashing the call history in front of Rivanah. The latter read on quickly. Nitya, Nitya, Nitya . . . some other names . . . couple of random numbers . . . not Nivan's.

'How much longer?' Nitya asked.

'Did you delete any number, Danny?' Rivanah asked.

'I really think you should visit a shrink, girl,' Nitya said.

'Excuse me, but I'm not talking to you,' Rivanah said, looking from Nitya to Danny.

'I too think you need to visit a shrink,' Danny said. Nitya almost pulled him inside. Did he delete the number or did he really not have any idea why she wanted to check his phone? A frustrated Rivanah left Boveda.

Half an hour later, she was in her flat in the Residency Enclave. Sitting on her bed, she had no clue what she should do next. Was it really supposed to end this way? The Stranger withdrawing without any notice after revealing what a bitch she had been to Hiya? The Stranger was still in touch with Nivan, then why not her? Why did the Stranger choose to talk in Danny's voice? Was Danny even speaking the truth? If he had deleted the number, she would never know. And she couldn't approach him again. Especially after the way both he and Nitya had treated her some time back. Rivanah lifted her head up and her eyes fell on the sketch stand. Hiya's face was half covered with something. She frowned. It was an A4 sheet. In fact, there were two sheets stapled together and taped to one edge of the sketch. Rivanah took it out. It read like a chat transcript between two people: the Stranger and Hiya. Before she could begin reading, something occurred to her and she rushed to the main gate. In two minutes, she reached the security guard's room. She checked the visitors' book but there was no entry mentioning a visitor to her flat. She asked the guard to show her the CCTV footage of her floor. Every corner of the Residency Enclave was under CCTV surveillance 24/7. As the guard played the footage for the day, Rivanah sat still beside him, staring unblinkingly at the screen. She could see the newspaper man, the sweepers and some residents coming into view and moving out. She saw Nivan leaving for work. She saw herself as well. She slowly started forwarding the footage until she stopped at a particular segment. Time 14.06. Someone had entered her flat through the front door and a minute later had stepped out. The person was wearing a cap, shades, jeans and a tight-fitting tee. Rivanah had made love to this man several times. How could she mistake him for anyone else? She paused the frame just before the person was about to enter the elevator.

'Do you know the person, madam?' the security guard asked, as Rivanah stared at the frozen image of Danny speechlessly.

33

It was late. Rivanah walked to Nivan's door but wasn't sure if she should ring the doorbell this late in the night. She decided against it and settled on her couch, clutching the chat transcript in her hand. Finally, she knew who the Stranger was. She read through the transcript in her hand.

Hiya: I know you did something so I couldn't go to the college on time. Tell me, what did you do?

Stranger: I didn't do anything.

Hiya: Wrong. You did. I don't know why you are after my life.

Stranger: I only want you to know your worth, Hiya.

Hiya: Cut the bullshit. You want to kill me. You knew how badly I wanted this job. My family is looking up to me to secure the job and then sponsor my little brother's dialysis. You knew it, damn it, and still you didn't let me have it.

Stranger: As I said, I wasn't the one who stalled you from going to college today.

Hiya: What's the use of lying to me now? Whoever you are, just know that you've left me with no option other than the one I'm opting for now.

Stranger: Hold on, Hiya. Don't be presumptuous.

Hiya: I did whatever you asked me to. I thought you were a friend.

Stranger: Hiya, you won't do anything which upsets me.

Hiya: Go to hell.

Stranger: Let me come to you.

Hiya: I don't care any more.

Stranger: Hiya.

Stranger: Hiya?

Rivanah knew why Hiya didn't respond—the date and time of the message was printed in a corner. It was the same night that Hiya was found hanging in her room. Hiya died without knowing it was Rivanah who had mixed the sleeping pills in her coffee which made her wake up late. *Too late. Why does the Stranger—or Danny— want me to read this?* Rivanah tried to guess the answer. Was it because he didn't want her to feel guilty about the fact that she thought she led Hiya to kill herself? Had Hiya known it was Rivanah who mixed those sleeping pills, she would have been upset but probably not killed herself? She probably wrongly assumed the Stranger would lead her to her doom, and thus, burdened with the brother's medical condition, hanged herself? It could be true as much as it could be false. Whatever she guessed would only be an inference of the truth but not the truth itself. And the one who could tell her the truth was the Stranger—Danny—whom she couldn't contact. He had—cleverly—made sure of that by bringing Nitya into the picture earlier in the evening. But she could make sure he came to her. If he was the Stranger then Danny would definitely come to her. She eyed the last words of the Stranger to Hiya in the transcript: *Let me come to you*. And that sort of desperation happened because the Stranger was convinced Hiya would kill herself. Rivanah knew what she had to do to summon Danny to her on his own will. She had tried to do it once before too. But that was pretence. This time it won't be pretence.

The next day Rivanah was quiet in the office. Nivan asked her if she managed to get through to the Stranger, but she was cold about it. She did dial the stored phone numbers again but they were still suspended. After lunch, she got a phone call from Kamble saying he was busy that day and asked if she could meet up the next day. Rivanah confirmed she would.

In the evening, while going back to her flat, time and again she kept stretching her hand out of the cab and clicking random photographs of the traffic behind her using her phone—a total of five clicks. And as she kept checking the photographs, she broke into a smile. One biker was common in all the photographs. She was right. She was still being followed. It wasn't over yet. Rivanah intentionally got down in front of the Residency Enclave and walked inside. She sipped her tea by the huge French windows in the drawing room overlooking the sea in the distance. Then she asked one of the security guards to come up with the terrace keys. The moment the guard came, she told him she had to check her dish antenna and so wanted the door to the terrace to be unlocked. The guard unlocked the terrace for her and waited. She asked him to leave and said that she would call him when she is done. The Stranger wouldn't appear if the guard was there with her. As the guard left reluctantly, Rivanah went to the edge of the terrace. A fierce sea breeze hit her hard. She felt at peace. She was almost lost at the sight of the sea ahead when she heard the sound of the elevator coming from the main control room atop the terrace. Her hunch told her the elevator would stop at the sixteenth floor—it did. The same hunch told her the one inside would take the steps to the terrace and would stop by the main door. Rivanah didn't turn around but could feel a presence. Something hit her. She bent down and picked it up. There was a pebble in the piece of paper crumpled into a ball. She dropped the pebble and read the words on the paper:

You don't have to do it, Mini.

Finally, for once, she was ahead of the Stranger. Of Danny. She turned around but saw only darkness by the terrace door.

'Why don't you show yourself, Danny? I know it's you,' she said aloud.

Seconds later, another paper ball with a pebble in it reached her.

Everything has consequences, Mini. Revealing who I am will have its own share of consequences.

'Why are you still so cryptic? I thank you for making me realize what my blunder was. How I lead Hiya to kill herself, but I also want to thank you for helping me learn to live with my blunders.'

Hiya didn't get the job because of you. But she died because of me.

Rivanah had understood it while reading the chat transcript.

'But what is it all about? Who are you really? What did you gain by being Hiya's Stranger, then mine and Nivan's too? Why did you keep reminding Hiya and me to know our worth?'

Can't we end this without questions?

'No, we can't. This isn't the time to play games, Danny. I know you still love me. Whatever you did in the ATM at Kalyan or at Boveda was all an act. Wasn't it?'

A paper ball reached her after a while.

Yes, I love you, Mini.

Rivanah could have cried reading it. Finally, there was some hope in her life. The line reminded her of what Nivan had told her once about standing by your choices. Another paper ball hit her.

I shall ask you one more time. Think and answer, because this choice of yours and mine will affect lives. It will be a lot of responsibility for you if I show myself. Are you sure you can handle it?

'I'm dead sure I can handle whatever it is. Especially after whatever you have been helping me learn.'

I'm happy, Mini, that it was all worth it.

'I want to hug you, Danny. Right now.'

Not now. We are being watched. We meet tomorrow, 8 a.m. sharp, at the edge of Nariman Point.

Rivanah heard the terrace door close. Danny was gone. What made him say they were being watched? Why was he so secretive even when she knew his identity? Most importantly, why did Danny have to play the role of Stranger in her life?

One more night—she checked the time on her phone—ten hours to be precise. And things shall become clear once and for all. Sleep was a distant cry for her. She was awake till six in the morning. Then she took a bath, got ready and took a cab to Nariman Point—the tip of Marine Drive in South Mumbai. She reached at the spot ten minutes before time. There were a few people sitting at some distance on the cemented barricade of Marine Drive and some others walking and jogging on the sidetrack. She was the only one standing at the edge. The morning breeze strengthened the hope she felt when she had read that Danny still loved her. Rivanah felt a tap on her shoulder. She turned around in a flash.

'Hello, Mini, I'm your Stranger.'

34

Rivanah's jaw slowly fell open.

'What the—' she just began but was stopped by a finger on her lips.

'You don't get to talk today. Only I do,' the person said. Rivanah kept staring at him as if she was looking at him for the first time.

'This is more complex, sinister and pertinent than you can even imagine, Mini. And it has rules. None of this is random. None of this can be proved.'

The Stranger was finally right in front of her—in flesh and blood. It was a face all too familiar for her. But how could it be . . .

'Firstly, I would like to apologize to you for those life-threatening attacks. My intention was never to kill you but I had to push you towards finding your link to Hiya because time was running out.'

'Time was running out? What do you mean?' Rivanah asked.

'We are a highly classified network of emotional-surgeons spread across the nation, working underground for a social revolution. Nobody knows how big or small the group is or who all are part of it. Believe me, even if your closest friend or family member has a Stranger in his or her life, he or she won't ever share it with you. We manipulate people in such a way that nobody has the option to talk about us. Like you too couldn't talk about me to many. Even if you did, there was no substantial evidence. We are the best-kept secret for the public at large. Our own statistic is that every seven-hundredth youngster in India has a Stranger in his or her life, as we speak. We are committed to raising the number.'

'What do you mean by "emotional surgeon"?' Rivanah mumbled. She was still trying to absorb it all. He looked at the sea in front and said, 'One of the weakest things about humans is we can be easily influenced. We are inherently gullible though we are one of the most intelligent creatures. This weakness is our group's strength. We initiate a change in people by influencing them. We don't perform physical surgeries on our targets but we work on their emotions. We push them to the edge. And we work within a time frame. We famish them emotionally as much as we nourish them. We alter their way of thinking, of perceiving things, their beliefs, their conclusions—in short, we alter them as an individual. You know, Mini, our everyday fight is between what we are holding on to and what we are letting go of. What we let go of changes us, what we hold on to alters us. Changes are irreversible. Alternations aren't.'

Like you initiated an alteration in me the first time I landed in Mumbai, Rivanah thought.

'Our social revolution is all about crushing that individual self in us, which is a product of a myopic and materialistic society, and knowing our real worth. If one observes people, one will know that people can be categorized, because there's a pattern—nobody is exclusive. Why do you think these social-networking platforms are a hit? Because deep down, we all are lonely, bitter and depressed. The extent varies, the extent of acceptance varies but we are these things. We all feel an urgent need to connect, to communicate without filters all the time, and yet we tell ourselves it isn't possible. That's where we emotional-surgeons come in. We pick our targets, we clean their bitterness by making them accept their deep-rooted mistakes, blunders which otherwise they would never embrace and always try to run away from. We sweep away their loneliness by explaining to them why one must love one's own self in the garb of the "share your good luck" endeavour.'

Like you made me learn to cook when I was depressed, you made me teach those slum kids and find happiness in simple things, you made me offer money to Mr Rawat, which told me I wasn't a bad person, after all.

'Everything needs time. Even sunlight needs time to explain to the seed why it is falling on it. The kind of social design we have knitted over years trains us subliminally to see things not as they are, but as we are told they are—no questions, no objectivity. We emotional-surgeons push people to question, to doubt their subjectivity, because otherwise, it makes our emotional selves blind with time. I too was made a part of it after being pursued by a year and a half by a Stranger who wanted me to know my worth. Not everyone we pursue is made a part of our group. But the ones who are—like I was—are given a target. Hiya Chowdhury was my first target. I had to perform an emotional surgery on her so that she could take on life better and realize her potential to the fullest. Our meticulous and collective planning is our strength. And my surgery on Hiya would have been successful had you not interfered, Mini. You drugged Hiya and she thought it was my doing. Before I could reach her, she had hanged herself assuming that I was some lunatic stalker harassing her.'

Nivan had both his hands in his trousers' pockets as he talked.

'But what about Danny's number in your phone labelled as Stranger?'

'He wasn't my Stranger. I was his. I'd recently started pursuing him, after the way he behaved with you inside the ATM in Kalyan. How do you think he cracked a film deal this quickly?'

'We all have secrets to hide, Mini, truths to confess. Danny coming to drop the chat transcript at your place yesterday was my manipulation, just the way I made you

271

resign from your job, compelled you to go to Prateek's place and the like.'

Everything added up now. Danny looked anxious when he came out to smoke with me in Boveda, looking around all the time, Rivanah thought and asked, 'But why didn't you come clean in front of Hiya like you are coming clean right now? Or did you come out clean in front of every target of yours?'

He gave her a tight smile and said, 'No, we don't come out clean in front of anybody.' A few silent seconds later, he added, 'Remember, how I had made you breathless on your terrace in Kolkata?'

The holding of hands . . . the pressing of the mouth . . . the clipping of the nose . . . Rivanah nodded.

'That's what you made me feel as well. Acutely desperate. Love's power of influencing us is always more than our scope of understanding it. In the quest to alter you, I fell for you, Mini, though I always believed I would never fall for anyone except Advika.'

Rivanah's lips parted but no words came out.

'Initially, I was angry with you for snatching an opportunity from me to influence Hiya. That's why I had attacked you in your flat too, but I let you go . . .'

Rivanah remembered the night clearly when she was alone in her flat, waiting for Danny, but she was attacked instead, stripped to the bare minimum.

'Why did you let me go that night, Nivan?' she asked.

'Not every pain you want to let go of, Mini. Some you want to keep by your side and watch it grow, because you know you too shall grow with the pain. You are one such pain for me, Mini,' Nivan said.

Rivanah didn't how to react. The initial shock of seeing Nivan as the Stranger had somewhat died down, but she wasn't ready for the fact that Nivan could actually love her. It was always supposed to be a fantasy. Or was this a fantasy?

'I could have told you on the first day itself that you were made to forget about Hiya through hypnosis, but I had to make sure that first you had the necessary strength to take such a thing. One can take as much shit as possible, but when it comes to one's own shit, the mind works in a different way, activating the weirdest of defence mechanisms.'

There was silence.

'Will you . . .' Rivanah stopped, feeling choked, and started again, 'Will you believe it if I say I love you, Nivan?'

'I know it, Mini.'

'What about Advika?' she asked.

The way Nivan looked at her first and then away, she knew their dilemma was the same.

'What happens next?' she asked.

'Next is this.' Nivan took out a piece of paper from his trousers' pocket and gave it to Rivanah. She was about to open its fold when Nivan stopped her.

'Not now. Before you read it, you have to listen to me carefully. I have played a big gamble on you. Don't you dare disappoint me on this, Mini.'

'What is it, Nivan?' she asked. She had a bad feeling about it.

'I told you there are rules in the world I'm a part of and one has to stick to those rules, come what may. And the foremost rule is a Stranger can't appear in front of his or her target. Come. What. May. I have already broken that rule for you, Mini. Thus there will be a price for me to pay.'

'What's the price?' The bad feeling in her guts became worse.

'It's in the note,' Nivan said, and in a flash took the note from her hand. He held it against the wind. He took out a lighter and set aflame one of the corners of the note as Rivanah watched in shock.

'Finish reading it before it all turns into ash. Don't follow me. Or call out to me. Whatever happens in the next minute happens because of me and not because of you. Remember that always and never be guilty about it. It was important for me to come clean in front of you,' Nivan said and planted a kiss on her lips, taking her by surprise. He turned and walked off. With a frown, Rivanah started reading the note which was slowly turning into ash. It read:

By the time you read the last word of this note, you'll know what I meant when I said last night that our meeting will have consequences. Ours is a doomed love story, Mini. And the doom is planned. I know of it. So does Advika. But she won't be able to deal with it alone. So she will be your responsibility from now on.

The rules of our underground group of Strangers are simple: if you know who we are, then you are one amongst us. Once you are in, you can't get out. If you don't comply, you are dead. You breach, you are dead. And our biggest strength is our secrecy because of which we convince people we don't exist. Like this paper shall turn to ash, swallowing all the words in it.

Don't let what you see when you are done reading this note break you in any way. In fact, don't react since we both are being watched right now. Any unfavourable reaction from your end, and they won't think twice before eliminating you. Someone will contact you in the next five days to tell you what's next for you. Accept it. Take care, Mini. Goodbye. We shall be together in some other life, maybe. This one was too complicated.

Rivanah let go of the paper as the fire licked the last bit up. As some of the ash slipped out of her hand, Rivanah heard a commotion at a distance. A car had run over someone. People had gathered. Rivanah wanted to throw up. She knelt by the edge of Nariman Point, trying to shut the noise around her. She could hear people screaming for someone to call the police. Her phone rang next. It was Inspector Kamble. She didn't take the call. He called again. She picked up.

'Rivanah, are you coming to meet me today?'

'I'm sorry, sir.' She was finding it difficult to talk. 'I'm out of the city right now.'

'Oh, not a problem. Let me get this done on the phone itself. I wanted to tell you there's one more person who lodged an FIR a few days back, claiming someone was stalking him. A little investigation told me that this guy too received messages on white cloth like you once did. Are you still getting them?'

'No, sir. They stopped coming long back.'

'Hmm. Okay, that's all. Thanks. You carry on.'

Glancing at the last piece of ash of Nivan's note being swept off into the sea by the wind, his words came back to her: *Advika is your responsibility from now.* The dreadful feeling was actually an intuition. If she knew this was going to be the end, then she wouldn't have ever asked the Stranger to reveal himself. Rivanah wanted to see Nivan for one last time, but she knew she couldn't. *We are being watched,* he had written. She stood up, hailed a cab and headed to the Residency Enclave, breaking down inside the car.

It took an hour and a half for her to reach her destination. She took the elevator and reached the sixteenth floor in no time. Standing in front of 1603, she was trying hard to not think of how she would react or in what state she would find Advika in. The servant opened the door and gestured towards the bedroom immediately. Xeno was sitting in a corner.

Rivanah went towards the bedroom. As she stood by the door, she could see Advika sitting by her window, looking out at the sea. Rivanah approached her with heavy steps. Once there, she placed a trembling hand on Advika's shoulder. The latter turned. Her eyes were swollen. Rivanah understood that Nivan must have told her about it beforehand. Advika threw a hand around Rivanah's waist and hugged her tightly. As she felt her body shudder against hers, Rivanah put her arms around Advika holding back her own tears. From someone who was always in need of a shoulder to cry on, the Stranger had turned Rivanah into someone who could lend a shoulder to someone in need. And for that, she would be forever indebted to Nivan . . . to her Stranger, whom she would never forget.

Epilogue

11 MONTHS LATER

Indigo flight 6E-332, Mumbai to Kolkata, 12.30 a.m.

Manish Agarwal switched on his mobile phone even before the flight had landed. He knew it was against the rules, but he didn't care. One after another, messages started pouring in on different social platforms. One of his close friends had sent him a dirty MMS on WhatsApp. It was of a girl giving a guy a blowjob. The next message read: *Rohit: 13. Manish: 11*, followed by a devil's emoticon.

Pretty soon, I'll up my score, asshole! Manish replied.

He looked up to see the air hostess he had been fantasizing about all through the flight. Her name tag read: Anita. Manish gave her a big toothy grin. She smiled back at him awkwardly.

After the exit doors opened, passengers started moving out of the aircraft with their luggage. As Manish reached the exit, he looked at the same air hostess who was now standing beside the door.

'Have a pleasant night, sir,' Anita said in the typical I-am-programmed-to-say-this manner.

Manish stopped and looking at her said, 'What are you doing later tonight?'

'Excuse me, sir?' Anita wasn't expecting it.

'Okay, let me be straight. Are you free to hook up tonight?'

'What do you think of yourself?' Her raised voice made others shoot a suspicious glance at Manish. It made him uncomfortable and also pinched his ego.

'I'll have to file a complaint against you if you repeat it,' Anita shot back.

Manish gave her an angry look and stepped out of the airplane. He was walking furiously on the aerobridge as he called his father.

'Manu beta, has your flight landed? I have already sent the new Jaguar to fetch you,' Mr Agarwal said. He was the largest sponsor for the ruling party in the state.

'I need to get an air hostess fired. Right. Now.' Manish was fuming.

'Oh. What happened?'

'I will tell you later. She needs to be fired first.'

'I'll see to it. You come home first.'

Manish cut the call and promised himself he would make Anita his bitch in no time.

After collecting his luggage, he pushed the trolley to the men's washroom to take a dump. Stepping in, he tried to locate the light buttons since the toilet was concealed in utter darkness. Before he could find it, someone held him by his collar and pulled him right inside one of the toilets. The door was pushed closed while his hand was held behind and twisted hard. Manish opened his mouth to scream but a sock was stuffed inside his mouth. There was a strong smell of some deodorant. Manish didn't know it was Just Different, Hugo Boss. Manish tried hard, but couldn't free himself from the tight grasp. It all happened in a way he had only seen in Bruce Lee films. It was evident that the attacker, whoever it was, knew martial arts. He felt something on his groin.

'That's a nutcracker right between your legs,' a girl spoke in his ears. 'Tell me, are you going to listen carefully to what I'm going to say or . . .' Manish nodded out of fear.

'Good. You will take the next flight back to Mumbai right now. The ticket is inside a packet by the washbasin outside. And when the flight takes off, you will hold your ears and do ten squats before Anita, the air hostess, and apologize to her.'

Manish started fidgeting only to feel his arm being twisted even more. He stopped for his own good. He heard the girl's voice again.

'Or else, I will crush your nuts first and then every bone of your body.'

The sound of it made Manish freak out. He shrank like a timid dog.

'Did you get what I just said?'

Manish nodded.

'Will you be a good boy, Manu?'

Manish nodded again, sweating profusely by now.

She removed the sock from his mouth.

'Who the fuck are you?' he said, gasping for breath.

'Anonymity is power, Manu.'

'Huh? What do you mean?'

'You can call me . . . Stranger,' said Rivanah.

Acknowledgements

I have always dreaded the moment when, after working on the Stranger trilogy for three years, the time would come for me to move on to a different story. The Stranger trilogy has been an educational journey for me. It was a deeply emotional experience as well. And as is true for every journey, there are always souls to thank when it comes to an end.

First and foremost comes my publisher, Milee Ashwarya; my editor, Gurveen Chadha; Shruti Katoch from Marketing; Rahul Dixit from Sales; and to each and every one in Penguin Random House who has shown faith in my work and supported me in presenting the trilogy to my readers. Heartfelt thanks, a loud cheer to you all!

Authors are mostly selfish about their work. And to balance it out, one needs a selfless family. My sincere respects and gratitude to my family for being there whenever I need them.

Since I'm a borderline social recluse, I would also like to thank the few friends I have, for being there, for inspiring me, for teaching me, rectifying me in innumerable ways, and supporting me too. Arindam, Rahul, Rachit, Arpit and Reetika: double thumbs-up!

Acknowledgements

Then there are people with whom you can't define your relationship, because it is a lot of everything and a little of nothing. Yet, you learn so much. Ranisa, Pauli, Anuradha, Siddhi, Pallavi, Trisha, Titiksha and Rashi: you guys may not realize it, but I've learnt a lot from you people, especially over the last one year. Thank you!

Pallavi Jha: as the trilogy draws to a conclusion, I thank you once again for planting the seed of the concept (though unknowingly!) in my head during one of our innumerable phone calls. I hope you continue to be happy and blessed. Here's to many more phone calls, cheers!

R, for . . . guess I should rest my words for once and let the dots take over . . . for it's in the dots that we define ourselves the best, isn't it?